THE BIG BOOK OF
Dancing Shoes

DANCING SHOES

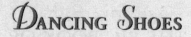

Other Dancing Shoes titles

Antonia Barber

The Big Book of
Dancing Shoes

Illustrated by Biz Hull

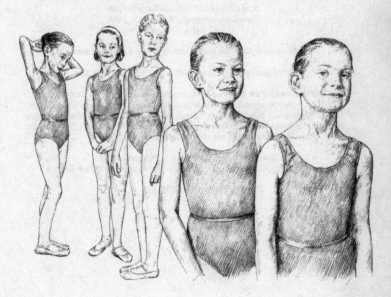

Published by the Penguin Group
Penguin Books Ltd, 27 Wrights Lane, London W8 5TZ, England
Penguin Putnam Inc., 375 Hudson Street, New York, New York 10014, USA
Penguin Books Australia Ltd, Ringwood, Victoria, Australia
Penguin Books Canada Ltd, 10 Alcorn Avenue, Toronto, Ontario, Canada M4V 3B2
Penguin Books (NZ) Ltd, Private Bag 102902, NSMC, Auckland, New Zealand

On the World Wide Web at: www.penguin.com

Penguin Books Ltd, Registered Offices: Harmondsworth, Middlesex, England

Lessons for Lucy first published in Puffin Books 1998
Into the Spotlight first published in Puffin Books 1998
Friends and Rivals first published in Puffin Books 1998
This edition published by Viking 2000
1 3 5 7 9 10 8 6 4 2

Text copyright © Antonia Barber, 1998
Illustrations copyright © Biz Hull, 1998
All rights reserved

The moral right of the author and illustrator has been asserted

Printed and bound in Great Britain by The Bath Press, Bath

British Library Cataloguing in Publication Data
A CIP catalogue record for this book is available from the British Library

ISBN 0–670–89356–0

Contents

Contents

Antonia Barber

Dancing Shoes
Lessons for Lucy

Illustrated by Biz Hull

Chapter One

'Why can't I look after Soggybottom? He's used to me and he's asleep anyway.'

   'Because you are too young to be left on your own.' Lou's mother flicked at her eyelashes with a small mascara brush and frowned into the mirror.

   'Why are you putting on eye make-up if you are only going to evening class?'

'I don't know . . . because when I look good, I feel clever. It's not easy going back to school when you're grown up.'

'Why can't Mrs Baines come, same as usual?'

'Because her mother is ill and she can't leave her.'

'Will she be ill for long?'

'How do I know?' Jenny Lambert ran a comb through her hair, scowled at the result and then smiled suddenly at her daughter. 'Come on, Lou, don't give me a hard time. Mrs Dillon is all right when you get to know her.'

Lou wasn't so sure. She was a bit scared of the old lady on the top floor. She talked oddly, she wore dark, dreary clothes and her hair always looked as if she had been out in a high wind.

'She smells funny,' she said.

'She uses an old-fashioned scent,' said her mother patiently, gathering up her files and folders. 'Have you got a pen, Lou?'

Lou did have a pen which she had borrowed from her mother's bag that morning, so it seemed only fair to give it back.

'We never used to talk to her,' she protested, hunting in her pencil case.

'Well, she liked to keep herself to herself, as they say. But when we had all that trouble with the landlord, we had to get together.'

'Is it all right now?'

'What?' Her mother took a quick peep into Charlie's room to see if he was still sleeping.

'The thing with the landlord. I mean, we don't have to move after all, do we?'

Her mother sighed. 'Well, he managed to sell the house without getting us out. We shall have to wait and see what the new owners are like.'

'Is it only for one night?' asked Lou.

'I can put up with Mrs Thing if it's only for tonight.'

'Now listen to me, Lucy.' Her mother went all solemn. 'If I don't do these classes, I won't pass my exam. If I don't pass my exam, I won't get a better job.' Her voice was rising ominously. 'And if I don't get a better job, I can't afford those gymnastics classes you are always on about. So, just get off my back, will you!' Her voice dropped back to its usual mild tone as she added, 'We're lucky to get a baby-sitter at all at the rates I can afford.'

Lucy gave in. She did want the gymnastics classes so badly. Every time Melanie Jackson turned somersaults in the playground or walked on her hands, she felt green with envy. Melanie had been doing gymnastics for two years and was very fond of showing off her skills. In her dreams, Lucy cartwheeled across the sports field, balanced with breathtaking poise along the beam in the gym hall and swung fearlessly from a trapeze. In her waking moments, she could not even walk on her hands without falling over.

'All right, all right,' she said hastily. She had remembered that there were two of her favourite programmes to watch on television, so she wouldn't have to spend much time talking to the old lady.

Chapter Two

'She is very pretty girl, your mother.' Mrs Dillon stood at the window watching as Jenny ran up the steps and turned along the avenue. She glanced down through the railings and the old lady moved her hand, as if to reassure her that all was well. 'Is good she goes out to this classes,' she said. 'She is young woman still. Is not good she is alone.'

'She's not alone,' said Lou crossly. 'She's got me and Soggybottom.'

'Who is this Saggingbottom?' The old lady sounded disapproving. 'Do I know this person?'

'Oh, that's Charlie,' said Lou, turning on the television. 'He's not really soggy any more, but that's what Dad used to call him.' She wished she hadn't said it. She didn't like talking about Dad to strangers.

'Is very bad thing to lose your father,' said Mrs Dillon, shaking her head as if it was Lou's fault. 'Is not good for a young widow to be left alone with children.'

'I don't talk about it,' said Lou in a grumpy voice.

'That I understand,' said Mrs Dillon.

'I also have sadness in my life.' For a moment she went on shaking her head thoughtfully at her memories. Then she said, 'We will watch beautiful television now and be happy again.' She reached out a long, thin finger and poked it into the television set, changing the channel.

Lou was horrified. 'I always watch *Ambleside* next,' she said and changed it back.

'Not always,' said Mrs Dillon firmly. Her finger struck again and the hills and vales of Ambleside gave way to heavy red and gold curtains filling a carved and gilded stage. 'Tonight we watch ballet.'

Lou was dumbstruck. Mrs Baines had always watched *Ambleside* with her and had chatted about the people in it

as if they were old friends. She
considered changing the programme
back again, but there was something
witch-like about the old lady's long
finger. She had an uneasy feeling that if

it pointed at her, she might turn into a frog. She could picture herself croaking pathetically on the armchair until Mrs Dillon's programme was over, and being changed back only at the last minute, as her mother came down the steps. She hunched up her shoulders, slumped back in her chair and sulked.

Mrs Dillon did not seem to notice. Nothing was happening on the screen. The red curtains were still closed, which was annoying because Lou could not help wondering what lay behind them. There was music playing and the camera was having a good look at the musicians, but it wasn't very interesting. Lou wondered whether young Sally had made up her quarrel with Andy, the *Ambleside* vet, and whether the Lummoxes' prize herd really had got some terrible disease.

Suddenly the music changed and the great curtains were swept aside. The whole stage was alive with movement and colour and the music seemed to fill Lou's head. A sword fight broke out; she sat up a little. Mrs Dillon glanced sideways and Lou thought she saw a tiny smile at the corner of her mouth. This made her feel very cross, as if the old lady had known that she would not be able to resist it. She settled back into her sulking position again and tried to pretend that she was not watching.

'Is *Romeo and Juliet*,' said Mrs Dillon. 'You know this story?'

Lou only knew that they were famous for being in love.

''Course I do,' she said. A rather handsome young man was leaping about with a sword, hogging the centre of the stage. 'That's Romeo,' she said, to show how well she knew it.

'No, that is Romeo's friend,' said Mrs Dillon. 'He is wild boy; Romeo is more quiet.'

Someone in gorgeous robes swept on and broke up the fight, which was a shame as Lou was just beginning to enjoy it. Then Romeo came on and, although he did not say a word, you could tell at once that he was pining.

'He is in love with the fair Rosaline,' explained Mrs Dillon.

Lou knew this must be wrong, so she said, 'Then why isn't it called *Romeo and Rosaline*?'

Mrs Dillon sighed. 'First, he is in love with Rosaline, then he is in love with Juliet. First love is little love; second love is BIG love.'

'He's not very faithful then?' said Lou rather primly.

'He is hot-blooded young man!' said Mrs Dillon scornfully. 'What you expect?'

Lou was beginning to find the whole evening rather exciting. Her mother never talked to her about hot-blooded young men.

Then Juliet appeared. Shy and yet eager, excited but nervous at her first ball, her slender white figure came down a grand flight of stairs and walked straight into Lou's heart. She could see, at once, why Romeo lost interest in the rather showy Rosaline. Watching her, Lou felt as if she had become Juliet. She seemed to see through her eyes, to feel all her wonder and delight. She felt as if she danced upon those slender, skilful feet.

Watching Juliet poised upon one toe, Lou said wistfully, 'Melanie Jackson can balance on one leg. She does gymnastics.' She was about to add that she too would be taking gym classes next year, but luckily she paused for a moment.

Mrs Dillon said, 'Gymnastics? Pouff! It is for circus performers!'

Lou had rarely been so shocked in all of her young life.

'Where is art? Where is beauty?' continued the old lady, never taking her

eyes from the television screen. 'Where is ROMANCE?' Then she repeated 'Gymnastics? POUFF!' rather as if she were blowing away a feather that had stuck to the end of her nose.

As her stunned mind came alive again, Lou suddenly saw that Mrs

Dillon was right. Melanie Jackson was clever, skilful even, but where was art? Where was beauty? And as for romance . . . She pictured herself saying to Melanie Jackson, 'Gymnastics? Pouff! It is for circus performers!' The very idea filled her with a wild glee, though she knew that she would never dare to do it. Melanie was thin, but her training had made her very wiry and tough. If I do gymnastics, she thought, Melanie will always be two years ahead of me. But if I do ballet . . .

Gymnastics was little love, she said to herself, ballet is BIG LOVE. She smiled one of her best smiles at Mrs Dillon (who didn't seem to notice) and went back to being Juliet.

Chapter Three

'Ballet lessons? BALLET LESSONS!
You must be joking!' Lou's mother's
voice drifted through from the tiny
kitchen, where she was doing
something noisy with a pan full of
potatoes.

'But, Mum . . .' said Lou. Charlie
was trying to scribble on the edge of
her homework.

'I've promised you gym classes, but I

can't afford any more!' The potatoes were getting a violent mashing.

'I meant "instead of",' explained Lou, 'not "as well as".'

'Instead of *gymnastics*? But you've been on about it for the last year. Honestly, Lou, you never stick to anything.'

'I yam hot-blooded young girl, vot you eggspect?' muttered Lou in Mrs Dillon's heavy accent. But aloud she said, 'Gym is OK but, I mean, it's just exercises, isn't it? There's no romance . . .'

'ROMANCE!' Lou's mother's face peered anxiously around the door. 'I don't want to hear that word for at least ten years,' she said hopefully.

'*Story* romance, not *sloppy* romance,'

said Lou scornfully. 'Shall I lay the table?' She gathered up her books and took her red felt pen away from Charlie, who was decorating his face.

As they sat down to sausages and mash, she tried to make her mother understand. 'I watched this ballet last night, Mum, with Mrs Dillon, and it was magic (*munch, munch*). There was Juliet and she was all shy and sort of breathless (*swallow*). See, it was her first ball and she was so light . . . she just floated about. I mean, gym is all right (*munch, munch*), but Melanie just sort of struts and sticks her bottom out (*swallow*) as if she was saying, "Look at me. Aren't I clever?" . . . But with ballet you can say all kinds of things . . . oh, I can't really explain it!'

'You're doing pretty well,' said her mother gently. 'Here, have another sausage.'

When evening class came round again, Lou looked to see if there was another ballet on television. There wasn't, but

Mrs Dillon surprised her. She rooted around in her shapeless brown bag and brought out a video cassette.

'You understand such things?' she asked Lou. 'You have a machine for making them work?'

'It makes them work sometimes,' said Lou.

The video cassette recorder was a luxury left over from the days when Dad was around. It was definitely past its sell-by date.

'I am getting this from the video shop,' said Mrs Dillon. She made it sound like a brave and risky thing to have done. 'It is *Giselle*.'

This time Lou didn't pretend she knew the story.

'Is very tragic tale of young girl who

dies for love,' said Mrs Dillon gloomily, as the ballet opened on a cheerful scene of peasants dancing.

The picture shimmered and broke up, but Lou gave it a quick expert thump and it settled down again. Giselle was the best of the dancers. She seemed hardly to touch the ground as she circled the stage. Lou sat entranced as the story unfolded. And all the time she hugged her great secret, thinking how impressed Mrs Dillon would be. At last she could wait no longer. 'I shall be starting ballet lessons next year!' she announced.

Mrs Dillon did not even take her eyes from the screen. 'Next year is too late,' she said. 'For myself, I began when I was four years old.'

25

Lou turned in astonishment. 'You did ballet?' she said, staring at the dowdy brown figure with the wild bird's-nest hair.

Mrs Dillon narrowed her eyes. 'And why not?' she demanded. 'I danced with the Bolshoi, the most famous ballet company in all Russia . . . in the world!'

Giselle, who had been crossed in love, was going gracefully mad on the screen.

Lou knew what must have happened. Old people sometimes got a bit odd, like the man in the park who talked to himself. Mrs Dillon had probably watched too much ballet and was now as mad as Giselle.

'I expect you were very good,' said Lou soothingly.

'I was *brilliant*,' said Mrs Dillon with a smug smile.

Lou could think of no answer to this.

When the first act of the ballet was over, she asked, 'Is it really too late for me?'

Mrs Dillon looked at her searchingly. 'Perhaps not,' she said, 'if you want it very much. But you must begin at once.'

'I can't,' said Lou miserably. 'We can't afford it until Mum gets a new job.'

'Ah . . . money.' Mrs Dillon nodded. 'It is always a problem.'

They watched the second half of the ballet without speaking. Giselle rose from her grave and joined a band of avenging spirits in long white dresses, but the thrill had gone out of it. Even

27

when she managed to save the life of her faithless lover, it did little to cheer them up.

'It is more than he deserved,' said Mrs Dillon drily, 'but women are fools for love.'

Lou nodded. 'That's what Mrs Baines says.'

'Best to stick to ballet,' said Mrs Dillon.

Lou didn't quite understand this remark. She had no intention of dying for love but felt that she might well die for want of ballet lessons. 'How can I stick to ballet', she moaned, 'when I can't even get started?'

Mrs Dillon frowned, then looked at her thoughtfully. 'Take off your shoes,' she said.

Taken aback, Lou did as she was told.

'Stand up, feet together.'

Lou stood up.

'Toes apart. Don't roll your ankles,' said Mrs Dillon and looked closely at Lou's feet.

Lou hunched her shoulders awkwardly.

'Stand tall! Raise your chin, shoulders down, bottom in . . . and don't wriggle!'

The orders came sharply, one after the other, and as she spoke the old woman circled around Lou, looking her up and down like a farmer pricing cows in a cattle market. At last she said, 'Humph!' and then, 'Sing to me.'

Lou dithered. 'What shall I sing?'

'Anything!'

Nervously she began to sing a pop song.

'Clap while you sing!'

This is getting really silly, thought Lou, but she clapped away.

'Enough!' said Mrs Dillon after a few minutes. She sat down and Lou stood facing her. 'First,' said the old lady, 'feet are good. That is important. Second, shape is good, but you do not stand well . . . we will change that. Third, you have ear for music and you feel the rhythm.'

As she spoke, Lou heard footsteps outside and the sound of the key in the lock.

'It is your mother,' said Mrs Dillon. 'I speak to her and, if she agrees, I will teach you to dance.'

Chapter Four

First position. Lou put her heels
together and turned her toes outwards
until her feet were in a straight line. Her
knees wobbled forwards, her bottom
wobbled backwards and she fell over.
She studied the book again. It was
called *Your Ballet Class* and she had got
it from the library. She tried to put her
feet like the dancer in the picture and
fell over again. Mrs Dillon said she

must put her feet at right angles to begin with. She said ballet dancers must learn to turn their legs and feet outwards a little more each day. But Lou was in a hurry. If I had started when I was four, she thought anxiously, I'd be able to do it by now! The odd thing was that Mrs Dillon could do it, in spite of being old and untidy and not a bit like a ballet dancer.

'Did she really dance with the Bolshoi?' she had asked her mother after the two women had been closeted together in Mrs Dillon's room.

'Yes, it seems so. It's really very kind of her to teach you. I can't pay her anything.'

'Why is she in England?'

'She came from Russia on a tour

with the Bolshoi and stayed behind.'

'But why?' Lou could not imagine any dancer leaving one of the greatest ballet companies in the world.

'She fell in love,' said her mother. 'She married an Englishman and gave up everything.'

Lou was speechless. 'Oh . . . wow!' she breathed. If there was anything more romantic than dancing with the Bolshoi, it was Giving It All Up For Love. She tried to picture Mrs Dillon, in her dull brown frock and sagging cardigan, as a Romantic Heroine, but it was even harder than imagining her as a Great Ballerina. And yet . . . she could turn her feet out without falling over.

Lou gave up first position and

decided to practise her *révérence*. Right foot forward, left leg behind, arms swept up sideways, knees bent into a graceful curtsy with head bowed. Then smoothly up again into a standing position. Mrs Dillon said she must do this at the beginning and end of every lesson. 'It is sign of respect,' she explained. 'The dancer thanks her teacher for giving her priceless knowledge.'

Lou tried to imagine the class at school curtsying to Jumbo Jones for giving them priceless maths.

She practised the *révérence* again, but raised her head, smiling at herself in the dingy mirror and lifting her right hand to accept the wild applause of a packed theatre. The reflection changed

from a skinny girl in a red bathing suit
to a prima ballerina in a white
embroidered tutu and a jewelled crown.
Then it changed back again.

The mirror was the door of an old
wardrobe. It had been left behind in the
empty bedroom of the flat upstairs,
which Lou was using as a practice
room.

A loud huffing and squeaking of brakes interrupted her dream. Peering through the torn net curtains, she saw that a big furniture van had pulled up outside. Some men opened up the back and settled themselves in a couple of armchairs with a flask of tea.

Lou's heart sank; the new owners had arrived. Now she would lose her practice room. Even worse, the new people might try to get them out again.

Lou gave up her ballet exercises and began dancing about with great leaps and twirls while she still had the space to do it. She was crossing the room on tiptoe, taking tiny delicate steps with her hands raised dreamily above her head and her eyes closed, when a voice said, 'You're awfully good.'

Lou fell off her toes and opened her eyes to see a pale, fair-haired girl of about her own age who gazed at her admiringly from the doorway.

'Have you been learning for a long time?' she asked wistfully.

Lou preened. 'Quite a while,' she said vaguely.

'I'm Emma Browne,' said the girl.
'Do you live here?'

'I'm Lucy Lambert. We live downstairs.'

'Is that your gran? The old lady I passed on the stairs?'

'No, I live with my mum and my brother, Charlie. Mrs Dillon lives on the top floor.'

'She's really weird!'

'She is a bit.' Lou felt she ought to defend Mrs Dillon but didn't have the courage.

'I've got a brother, called Martin. He's fourteen. How old is yours?'

'Nearly two,' sighed Lou, who had always wanted an older brother.

But the girl said, 'Oh, you are lucky! I wish we had a baby.'

'You can share if you like,' said Lou generously.

'Can I? Oh, great! You could share Martin, only he's away at boarding school most of the time, and when he is at home he's a real pain.'

'We could gang up on him,' said Lou, who quite liked sorting out stroppy boys.

Emma gave her a broad smile and edged a little further into the room. Lou did another twirl, hoping for some more admiration.

'Where do you have your ballet lessons?' asked Emma.

'Er . . . um . . .' said Lou. It would ruin her image to say 'from the weird old lady upstairs', so instead she said, 'At the Maple School of Ballet.' It

wasn't really a lie, she thought, because
she would be going in a year's time.

Emma's face lit up. 'Oh, brilliant!'
she said. 'I'm starting there next term.
We can go together.'

'Oh . . . great,' said Lou with rather
less enthusiasm. She could see that she
was going to have a problem.

Chapter Five

Lou sat on a stool in Mrs Browne's kitchen and told her all about the ballet class. The trouble with lies was that one led to another until it was hard to remember them all. And now, as she waited for Emma to come home, she was telling lies to Emma's mother.

It had all started when she had said that she went to the Maple School of Ballet. Emma had kept asking questions about it and Lou had had to make up the answers. She'd remembered the ballet book and talked confidently about satin shoes and leotards.

'What colour leotards?'

'Pale blue,' said Lou. She had seen the girls arriving for classes as she came home from school.

'Can I see yours?' asked Emma.

Lou had thought fast. 'It got too small,' she said. 'Mum took it to the charity shop. I'm having a new one next term.'

'Oh, good,' said Emma. 'We can go and buy them together.'

'Er . . . super!' said Lou.

'What is the ballet room like?'

Lou knew this from the book.

'Well . . . it's got one wall like a big mirror and a wooden bar to hold on to when we do our *pliés*.'

In fact she had to hold on to the back of a chair to do *pliés* for Mrs Dillon.

'What's a *plié*?'

Lou found a chair the right height. Holding on to it, she placed her feet

together, toes pointing outwards, and slowly bent her knees . . . down and then up again.

'Let me do it,' said Emma.

'You have to keep your head up and your back straight,' said Lou, trying to sound as if she had been doing *pliés* for years. Then she showed Emma first position and was pleased to find that she could turn her feet out more than Emma without falling over.

'I suppose that's because you've been doing it so much longer,' said Emma. 'Do you think I'll ever catch up? It would be fun if we were in the same class.'

Rather gloomily, Lou had agreed that it would. So far, with a bit of imagination, she had managed to keep up the pretence. But as soon as the term started, she knew the truth would come out.

Now Lou squirmed on Mrs Browne's kitchen stool as she thought about it.

Emma's mother had blue eyes and blonde hair that never moved. She was doing vegetables at the sink with pink rubber gloves on. Lou liked her a lot.

'I think that's really nice, curtsying to your teacher,' said Mrs Browne approvingly. 'I did tap when I was a little girl, but we just mucked about and giggled a lot. I often wish I'd taken it seriously.' As she emptied the sink and peeled off the rubber gloves, she said, 'It's really kind of your mother to have Emma tomorrow night. It's our wedding anniversary and Peter is taking

46

me somewhere really special.'

Lou turned pale. 'But it's Mum's evening class tomorrow,' she said.

'Yes, I know, but she said your baby-sitter wouldn't mind.'

'But . . . Mrs Dillon has already got me and Charlie to look after and . . . and she does get a bit muddled.' This was a truly awful lie and Lou turned from pale to pink.

Mrs Browne looked anxious. 'Does she? Maybe I should have a word with Jenny.'

'No . . . No!' Lou backtracked. 'She doesn't actually get muddled . . . I mean . . . she gets her English a bit mixed up.'

Mrs Browne looked relieved. 'Oh, that's no problem, and I'm getting you a ballet from the video shop.' She glanced at her little gold watch. 'Emma should be home from her piano lesson any minute.'

'Oh . . .' said Lou. 'I just remembered something. Tell her I'll be back soon.'

She raced up the stairs with a horrible sick feeling in her stomach. The whole deception was going to fall about her ears. She knew she would be found out in the end, but this was much too soon. If she and Emma had time to become close friends, well . . . she might be able to confess and make a joke about it . . . but not yet!

Mrs Dillon opened her door to find a very breathless, worried Lou outside.

'Something is wrong?' she asked. 'Your mother is needing me?'

Lou tried to look casual. 'No . . .

no . . .' she said. 'It's about tomorrow.'

'Ah, yes. Mrs Browne's little girl will join us. We shall watch *The Nutcracker*.'

'I don't want a lesson,' said Lou quickly. 'I mean, there won't be time . . . I mean, I don't want Emma to know . . . about the lessons.'

Mrs Dillon frowned. 'And why is that?'

Lou felt her face burn. 'It's . . . it's a secret,' she said lamely.

Mrs Dillon looked at her for a long time. 'Ah,' she said at last, 'a secret. Then, of course, I shall say nothing.' And she turned away with great dignity and closed the door.

Chapter Six

Lou felt like a cat on a hot tin roof. She had fed *The Nutcracker* into the gaping mouth of the video recorder and thumped the wavering picture. Now she sat on the sofa with Emma and Mrs Dillon and waited jumpily for one of them to give the whole game away. It would probably be Emma. Lou was pretty certain that Mrs Dillon would keep her word, that she would not mention the lessons. But the old lady seemed unusually quiet. She talked only enough to show that she was friendly to Emma, and Lou knew that she had offended her.

The Nutcracker opened with a splendid Christmas party. Guests were arriving and greeting one another, and there was a little girl who was shy and was hiding on the window seat, half hidden by a velvet curtain.

'That's just how I feel when my mum and dad have parties,' said Emma. 'I sort of like it, but I'd rather just watch the others.'

'I too was a shy child,' said Mrs Dillon.

Lou didn't believe it for a moment. She felt that Mrs Dillon was siding with

Emma to make her feel left out, that the old lady was punishing her. But that's stupid, she told herself. She's just being friendly because Emma doesn't know her.

The ballet had lots of children who danced about among the adults.

'Gosh!' said Emma. 'They're not much older than us. Fancy dancing on the stage in a proper ballet. They must have started lessons as soon as they were born!'

'They are older than they seem,' said Mrs Dillon knowingly, 'and the steps they do are simple. And you see that they do not dance on their toes.'

'I can stand on my toes,' said Emma eagerly.

'Is not good for young child.' Mrs

Dillon was very firm. 'Bones are still growing and you do not yet have proper shoes.'

Emma seemed relieved. 'Well, I always fall over after a couple of seconds,' she admitted. 'Perhaps I'll wait till I'm older.'

'That would be wise,' said Mrs Dillon approvingly.

Just chat among yourselves! thought Lou crossly. Don't mind me!

'I'm going to a ballet workshop next week,' said Emma proudly. 'It's a special holiday class for if you are starting next term . . . so you can get used to everything.'

'Which school is this?' asked Mrs Dillon.

'The Maple,' said Emma. 'But I already know a lot about it because Lou has told me.'

Lou slid down into the corner of the sofa and tried to hide behind a cushion.

'Ah,' said Mrs Dillon. 'This Maple is the school where Lou is also going?'

'Yes!' Emma's eager little voice grated on Lou like a knife on glass. 'Only, of course, Lou doesn't have to go to the Beginners' Workshop because she's been there for ages.'

'I do wish you'd stop talking,' shouted Lou desperately. 'I'm trying to watch the ballet!'

Emma looked wounded. Mrs Dillon raised her eyebrows. Charlie woke up and began to wail. Lou felt awful.

Mrs Dillon went to settle Charlie down and then returned to the sofa. For a long time nobody spoke. As time passed and still Mrs Dillon said nothing, Lou suddenly knew that the old lady would not show her up in front of Emma. But somehow that only made her feel worse.

The Nutcracker was beautiful, but Lou hated every minute of it. She wished she had never wanted to do ballet. She glanced at Emma, who was gazing at the screen, lost in the magic of it all. It was all right for her. She had a dad with enough money to buy a house and a mother with shiny pink nails and hair that never got out of place. She could have ballet lessons as soon as she asked for them, and piano lessons too. Lou hated Emma. And Mrs Dillon knew that she was a liar, and might guess why she had lied, and then she would like Emma best. So Lou hated Mrs Dillon too.

When *The Nutcracker* was over, Lou went to fetch milk and biscuits. She had to get away from the others somehow. While she was in the kitchen, Mrs Dillon turned to Emma. 'You are happy to be going to this ballet school?'

'Oh, yes!' said Emma. 'It will be great and I shall have Lou to go with. She's my best friend and I'm a bit nervous with strangers.'

'Yes,' said Mrs Dillon thoughtfully, 'is good to learn with others. There is discipline in a class, and friendship too. It will be good for both of you.'

She said nothing to Lou, who could not meet her eyes. She took the milk and biscuits and thanked her politely. But when she was back in her attic room, Mrs Dillon opened up her old desk and took out a sheet of thick, cream writing paper. She sat and stared at it for a while, then she began to write a letter.

Chapter Seven

The morning after next, Lou was
helping her mother to put a reluctant
Charlie into his push-chair when they
heard a loud ringing at the door
upstairs.

'The Brownes are out,' said Lou's
mum, struggling with the clips. 'See
what they want.'

Lou put her head out of the
basement door and called, 'Who is it?'

A large, breathless and, it seemed to Lou, rather excited lady came hurrying down the steps.

'Hello!' she said, in that special sort of voice some people keep for talking to children. 'Hello! Are you by any chance Lucy Lambert?'

'Yes,' said Lou cautiously.

'I guessed!' said the large lady. 'You have that quality about you . . . You are the little dancer!'

'I do a bit,' said Lou even more nervously.

'I', said the large lady proudly, 'am Miss Maple from the Maple School of Ballet.'

Lou panicked. She remembered suddenly that this was the day when Emma was doing her Beginners' Workshop. She guessed what had happened. Emma had told them that Lou had said she was a pupil there and now Miss Maple had hurried round in person to tell everyone that it wasn't true.

'Who is it?' Her mother's voice came

61

from inside, together with Charlie's, protesting as usual against the push-chair straps.

'No one!' said Lou quickly. 'I mean it's not important . . . just someone for the Brownes.'

'No . . . No,' said Miss Maple firmly. 'I have come to see Irina Barashkova.'

It was going to be all right, thought Lou hopefully. Miss Maple had just got the wrong house. 'There's no one here called that,' she said quickly. 'You've got the wrong address. Try down the street.'

If only she could get rid of the woman before her mother came out. But it was too late. Jenny bumped Charlie over the threshold and said, 'Irina Barashkova? Oh, that will be

Mrs Dillon. Ring the top bell.'

'I have rung it several times,' said Miss Maple, 'but there is no reply. I rang the lower bell to inquire whether, perhaps, she was away.'

'Lou will find out for you,' said her mother. 'Run upstairs, love, and see if Mrs Dillon is in.'

Lou bolted upstairs, thinking fast. She was still expecting some painful comeuppance. Miss Maple would tell Mrs Dillon that she had lied, or Mrs Dillon had already told Miss Maple and she would have to face them both. Everyone would get to hear about it, even the others at school. 'Liar! Liar! Pants on fire!' . . . She saw herself pursued home by a jeering mob. Her heart pounded with fear and the effort

of running up four flights of stairs. She banged on Mrs Dillon's door.

'Who is there?'

'It's me, Lou. There's a lady to see you. Miss Maple from the ballet school.'

'No . . . No! I cannot see her!' Mrs Dillon sounded as panicky as Lou.

'What shall I say?'

'I am not well! I can see no one! Please, go away.'

Lou felt as if the executioner had suddenly announced that he had left his axe at home.

'Don't worry,' she called cheerfully. 'I'll get rid of her.'

Mrs Dillon groaned from beyond the door.

In the basement, Miss Maple and her mother were deep in conversation. Lou arrived panting.

'She's not well. She can't see you. You've got to go away.'

'Lou!' said her mother. 'That's not very polite.' She turned back to Miss Maple. 'I'm so sorry,' she said, 'especially when you have been so kind. Could it wait until another day, while I go up and see if Madame Barashkova needs my help?'

'Of course . . . of course! Please do not trouble her . . . the artistic temperament . . . How well I understand it!' And, much to Lou's relief, the large lady bowed her way out up the basement steps.

When she had gone, her mother said, 'Well, Lou Lambert, and what do you suppose Miss Maple came about?'

Lou said nothing. She just waited for the sky to fall on her.

'She came . . .' said her mother slowly, 'she came . . . to offer you free lessons at the ballet school.'

Chapter Eight

Lou could hardly believe it. One minute
disaster was looming, then suddenly
she had her dearest wish. Instead of
being punished for all the lies, she
seemed to be being rewarded. Life was
very puzzling.

'Aren't you pleased?' asked her
mother.

'But why?' said Lou. 'I don't
understand it.'

'Well, it seems that Mrs Dillon wrote to the school. She told them that she was Irina Barashkova, who once danced with the Bolshoi. She said she had been teaching a very promising little girl who needed to be in a class with other children. She asked them to give you a scholarship, which means free lessons for a year.'

Lou was lost for words. At last she said, 'Mrs Dillon did that . . . for me?'

'Yes.' Her mother smiled. 'Wasn't it kind? And now it seems she's not very well, so keep an eye on Charlie while I pop up and see if she needs any shopping.'

Charlie was still strapped into his push-chair. To keep him amused, Lou danced for him, whirling and leaping as

best she could in the narrow space.
Charlie laughed a lot. He seemed to
find Lou's dancing very funny; he had
no taste!

When her mother came down again,
they set out for the street market where
they did their Saturday shopping. As

they walked along, Lou asked, 'Is Mrs Dillon very ill?'

'Well . . . no,' said her mother. 'To be honest, she's not really ill at all. But she is depressed . . . very sad . . . and she doesn't want to see anyone.'

'Why is she sad?'

'Well . . . when she was young, she was very beautiful and very talented. Now she is growing old and she feels that she has become drab and dowdy. She says that she doesn't want Miss Maple to see her, that she will never believe she was a Bolshoi dancer.'

Lou, who hadn't believed it herself, felt guilty.

'She seemed to think that even you were ashamed of her,' her mother went on, easing Charlie over the edge of the pavement, 'that you didn't want Emma to know she was giving you lessons.'

'Oh . . . that's not true!' said Lou, before she could stop herself. But she knew that it was true.

'That's what I told her. I said you were very proud to be having lessons from Irina Barashkova.'

'Yes . . . yes, I am,' said Lou in a small voice.

'I thought so.' Her mother looked down and gave her a funny smile. Lou's mouth smiled back.

She loved the street market. She loved the noise and the bustle, the stalls piled high with fruit and spices. She loved all the different people and the different smells, even the pongy smell of the fish stall. But today it had lost some of its magic. Lou kept thinking how kind Mrs Dillon had been to her and how mean she had been in return.

'Did Mrs Dillon need any shopping?' she asked.

'No,' said her mother. 'But I thought we might take her a little gift.'

She let Lou choose a bunch of violets from the flower stall and six hand-made chocolates in a little gold box.

They arrived back just as the Brownes' car returned from the supermarket. They were unloading a whole heap of bulging plastic carrier bags and Lou wondered how they would ever manage to eat it all. They were none of them very fat.

Mrs Browne greeted them cheerfully and, leaving her husband to finish the job, accepted Jenny's offer of a cup of coffee. The two women settled themselves in the kitchen, with Charlie sitting on Mrs Browne's lap and trying to chew her shiny pink fingernails.

'Shall I take these upstairs?' asked Lou, waving the flowers and the little gold box.

'Good idea,' said her mother.

This time Lou didn't run up the

stairs. She took her time, as she had to get her courage up. She knew what she had to do, but it was not going to be easy. She knocked on the door and called, 'Mrs Dillon. It's me, Lucy.'

The door opened cautiously.

'I came to say "thank you",' said Lou, 'for writing to the ballet school, I mean . . . and to bring you these.' She held up the gifts.

Mrs Dillon took them and stared at them and then said, 'Is very kind. I was pleased to help.'

But Lou wasn't finished. 'Only I don't want them,' she said. 'I mean the lessons at the ballet school. I'd much rather be taught by Reena Brushover. I mean . . . I'd be *really* proud.'

Mrs Dillon said nothing for a long

time. She looked a bit as if she might be going to cry, but then she smiled instead. She said, 'Lies are funny things: most are bad . . . but some are beautiful.'

Lou didn't understand, so she just smiled back.

'I will be proud to teach you,' said Mrs Dillon, 'but, you see, it is better for you to learn with others. There is more discipline in a class. Therefore, you must also go to the school.'

Lou's heart leapt with joy. 'Well, if you're quite sure,' she said eagerly.

'Quite sure,' said Mrs Dillon. 'And thank you for your lovely gifts.'

Lou went down the stairs two at a time.

Chapter Nine

When Emma got home that afternoon from the Beginners' Workshop, she was as excited as Lou. 'It was just like you said, the changing room and the ballet room and everything!'

'Great,' said Lou.

She had confessed everything to her mother: about how she had told the first lie and then had to make up more and more.

'You'll have to tell Emma in the end,' her mother had pointed out. 'She'll see when you start that you are in the beginners' class.'

'I know,' said Lou, 'but can I please tell her when *I'm* ready?'

She was not ready yet.

'We were all measured for our leotards,' said Emma. 'They are blue, just like you said . . . But you know all that, I don't know why I'm telling you.'

'Oh, that's OK,' said Lou carelessly. 'I quite like hearing about it.' In fact she was greedy for every detail.

'We don't have satin shoes with ribbons,' said Emma. (Bother! thought Lou. I got it wrong!) 'Well, not to start with. I expect you have them because you've been doing it longer. We have

soft leather shoes and my mum has got
to sew a bit of elastic across to stop
them coming off.'

'Did you do a *révérence*?' asked Lou.

'Oh, yes. She told us all about it, and
mine was one of the best because you
had shown me how. We had to do it in
front of the class so that the others
could see . . . oh, it was great!'

Lou suddenly felt very envious. She

was sure that her own *révérence* would have been one of the best if only she had been there. It was hard to put up with Emma's excitement when she couldn't show her own. But how could she share the good news that she was also going to the ballet school next term, when Emma thought she had been there for ages?

Something was going on in the house, but Lou could not make out what it was. The two mothers were in and out of each other's kitchens, deep in conversation. Then they both disappeared up to Mrs Dillon's flat and came out an hour later looking very pleased with themselves.

'What's going on?' asked Lou.

'Ask me no questions and I'll tell you no lies,' said her mother annoyingly.

When they went to the library on the Monday, Lou's mother said she had to call in at the charity shop. She parked Charlie in one corner and left Lou to amuse him while she ferreted through the racks. They came out with two bags.

'What is it?' asked Lou, peering into the larger one. It seemed to be a smart frock in a dark mauve colour. It wasn't the sort Jenny usually wore. 'Is it for special?'

Her mother grinned. 'Sort of . . .' she said.

The little bag held a rather nice leather belt. On the way back they popped into another charity shop and this time Jenny bought a heavy silk scarf. It was white with a pattern of flowers painted in lilac and pale green. Lou thought it was very pretty.

At the cake shop they stopped and bought a box of really posh cream cakes. Lou helped to choose them. 'Are we having a party?' she asked wonderingly.

'Miss Maple is coming to tea', said her mother, 'so that you can dance for her.'

A big thrill of excitement ran up Lou's spine. 'Dance for her?' she said nervously.

'Just a little, and do some of the ballet exercises Mrs Dillon has taught you. It's called an audition. And if she thinks you have promise, then you will have free lessons until I can afford to pay.'

'Suppose I haven't got promise?'

'Well, Irina Barashkova thinks you have and she should know.'

But was Mrs Dillon really Reena Brushover? thought Lou. Suppose it was just a fantasy and Miss Maple found out?

Back at the house, something was going on in the Brownes' bathroom. Emma met Lou at the door and dragged her upstairs. 'Guess what?' she breathed, her eyes wide with wonder.

'Tell me!' said Lou, who couldn't wait to guess.

'My mum is doing Mrs Dillon's hair!'

'Your mum . . .'

'Yes, she used to be a hairdresser, only my dad doesn't like her going out to work.'

'And she's doing Mrs Dillon's hair?'

'Yes.'

'Oh . . . wow!' said Lou. She tried to imagine what Mrs Browne might do to the bird's nest. She had a sudden picture of Mrs Dillon with bright blonde curls that never moved. Would that make her look more like Reena Brushover? Lou had terrible doubts.

They huddled outside the bathroom door, listening to the sound of low voices and water spraying.

'Push off, nosy ones!' Lou's mother came upstairs with the bags and caught them giggling and trying to look through the keyhole.

With shrieks of laughter, they escaped into Emma's bedroom.

'I really like your mum,' said Emma.

Lou liked her too, but wanted to
know why.

'Well, she says things like, "Push off,
nosy ones!"' explained Emma. 'My
mum would say, "Now, Emma, that's
not very nice, is it?"' She did a very
good imitation of Mrs Browne and they
both fell around laughing.

Chapter Ten

Miss Maple arrived promptly at four
o'clock. It had been decided that Lou
should audition first and that Emma
and Mrs Browne would join them for
tea at half-past four. Lou's mother
thought this would make Lou less
nervous, which was true, since she
could not explain to Emma why she
was doing the audition in the first place.

Lou was on tenterhooks. She sat and

wriggled while Miss Maple asked her which was her favourite ballet. '*Romeo and Juliet*,' said Lou, because Juliet was the part she most longed to dance.

Miss Maple seemed to be on tenterhooks too. She seemed to be listening to Lou with only half an ear. The other one and a half seemed to be listening for steps on the stairs, because Lou's mother had gone up to fetch Reena Brushover. What would Miss Maple think when she saw her? Lou pictured stiff blonde hair above the shapeless brown dress and sagging cardigan. Would Miss Maple think that Mrs Dillon was an impostor?

There were voices outside and the other door opened. For a moment Lou thought the woman with her mother was a stranger. Then Jenny said, 'Madame Barashkova, may I introduce Miss Penelope Maple of the Maple School of Ballet.'

The woman seemed somehow taller than Mrs Dillon. She wore a slim, plain dress of a dark mauve colour with a smart leather belt at the waist. Around her shoulders was draped a white silk scarf. It had a pattern of flowers in lilac and green and was pinned with a simple brooch at one side. Her hair wasn't blonde; it was a soft grey, parted in the middle and brushed back from her face like a real ballerina. It didn't have a bun at the back, though, but a rather elegant roll which made a lovely shape when she turned her head. She even had a little make-up around her eyes. Lou thought she looked lovely. There was no doubt about it: Mrs Dillon really was Reena Brushover!

'Madame Barashkova, this is such a pleasure!' Miss Maple had become all dithery. She looked as if she longed to do a *révérence*, but did not dare to do more than clasp the hand of the stately vision before her.

'I hear good things of this ballet school,' said Mrs Dillon graciously. She waved a hand at Lou. 'Is good that this child should go there.'

'I'm sure we should be delighted . . .' began Miss Maple, but Mrs Dillon cut her short with a firm, 'First, she is dancing for you, then you are deciding.'

Lou found that she was much more nervous of dancing for Reena

Brushover than for Miss Maple.

'Calm yourself, child,' said Mrs Dillon's familiar voice. 'We shall go through your usual lesson.'

She made her do three positions for her feet and three arm positions. Back straight, thought Lou, tummy in, head up. She tried to remember all the things she had been told: no elbows sticking out. 'Ballet dancers do not have elbows,' Mrs Dillon had insisted. When the exercises were completed, Mrs Dillon told Lou to dance freely. She had brought down a tape of the music for *Romeo and Juliet* and Lou danced her own version of Juliet at her first ball.

Mrs Dillon and Miss Maple talked while she danced. She heard words like 'improvisation' and 'musicality', but did

not know if they were good or bad.
Then the music stopped and Miss Maple
took Lou's hands. 'Madame Barashkova
is right,' she said. 'It will be good for us
to have you at the Maple School.'

Lou's mother hugged her and Lou
hugged Mrs Dillon. She almost hugged
Miss Maple too, but thought perhaps not.

'I'll make the tea now,' said Lou's

mother, 'while Lou goes upstairs to fetch Emma and Mrs Browne.' Outside the door she added, 'Tell Mrs Browne to come on down, while you have a private word with Emma.'

Lou knew what she meant. So she sent Mrs Browne downstairs and dragged Emma off to her bedroom, where they could be alone.

'What is it? . . . What is it?' asked Emma eagerly. She could see that Lou had something important to tell.

'It's a long story,' began Lou reluctantly.

'Go on, then.'

'Well . . . you know that first day you came . . . and I was dancing in the empty room . . . and you asked me . . .' And then she told Emma the whole story, all about the lies and how she had made it up about the ballet school, and about Mrs Dillon being Reena Brushover and everything. And Emma was so goggle-eyed that Lou found herself making the whole tale sound even sillier than it was. And Emma laughed and kept saying, 'Oh, Lou, you didn't!' and 'Wow! But how did you know about it?' and 'Lucy Lambert, you are really mad!'

'So you don't mind?' asked Lou, when Emma had stopped laughing.

'Mind?' said Emma. 'I think it's brilliant! It means we can start our classes together.'

'So it does,' said Lou. 'I hadn't thought about it like that.'

As they went downstairs, Emma said

wistfully, 'Everything happens to you, Lou, just like in a story. My life is really boring.'

'Not now,' said Lou. 'You're my best friend now.'

'Will that make a difference?' asked Emma. She sounded hopeful.

'More than likely,' said Lou.

And they went in together to see if the grown-ups had scoffed all the cream cakes.

Antonia Barber

DANCING SHOES
Into the Spotlight

Illustrated by Biz Hull

Chapter One

'It's not fair!' Lou put her chin down, pushed her chair back and sulked.

Her mother raised her eyebrows and went on trying to spoon food into Charlie, who quickly moved his head sideways. The food landed on his cheek and he looked hopefully at his sister to see if she would laugh. Lou didn't even notice.

'I don't see why Emma can't come to

our school,' she said. 'I mean, she wants to be at the same school as me, don't you, Emma?'

Emma had finished eating and sat with her elbows on the table and her chin in her hands. Her wide eyes switched anxiously from Lou to her mother and back as they argued. She felt really guilty because her parents were sending her to a private school instead of to the local school where Lou went.

Lou was her best friend. In fact, she was her only friend, because the Brownes had just moved into the area. Emma had been uprooted from the neat little house where she had grown up, because her dad had been promoted. They had moved to the centre of the city to this tall, run-down house which

Emma had hated at first. But then she found Lou and Lou's mother and Charlie living in the basement, and Mrs Dillon, who had once been a real ballet dancer, living in the attic.

Now she loved sharing a house with other people, and it seemed to her that her old life had been very dull. It was fun to go downstairs and have a meal with the Lamberts. Lou's mother was always too busy wrestling with Charlie to notice if Emma had her elbows on the table. Her own mother had eyes like a hawk and would have said, 'Now, Emma! Elbows, dear!'

'Don't you, Emma?' repeated Lou, frowning at her crossly.

Emma jumped, opened her eyes even wider and said hastily, 'Yes . . . yes, I do!'

But she wasn't at all sure what she was agreeing with.

'She doesn't want to go to that boring girls' school and wear that silly uniform, do you, Emma?'

'No, I –' began Emma, but Jenny Lambert interrupted her.

'It's a very smart uniform,' she said, 'and it's a good school, so don't start putting it down, Lou. Emma's parents want her to go there and that's the end of it.'

'But what's wrong with my school?' demanded Lou. 'Isn't mine a good school?'

'Yours is a very good school,' said her mother patiently as she wiped bits of food from Charlie's face, 'but Mr and Mrs Browne prefer the other one.'

'My mum doesn't mind,' said Emma.
'It's my dad . . . well, it's my granny
really. She sent my dad to a private
school, so she thinks they are better.'

'Well, they're not!' said Lou loudly.

'*I* didn't say they *were*,' protested
Emma. 'I just said that my gran . . .' She
felt close to tears. It was the first time she
had quarrelled with Lou . . .

'Now stop it, the pair of you!' Jenny Lambert broke in. She smiled at the two girls. 'Look,' she said, 'there are good and bad private schools, and there are good and bad state schools. Luckily you will both be going to good ones, and it's a really silly thing to quarrel about. After all, you will both be going to the same ballet school.'

This was a cunning move. She knew that if she could switch them on to the subject of ballet, the argument would end. Ballet was the strong bond that tied the two girls together, and they were both starting at the Maple School of Ballet as soon as the term began. There had been a bad time when it seemed that Emma would start without Lou. Jenny Lambert was a widow and she couldn't afford

Lou's ballet lessons yet. But Mrs Dillon, who lived upstairs, had once danced with the famous Russian Bolshoi Company. She had persuaded the owner of the ballet school, Miss Maple, to give Lou free lessons for a year.

Every time Lou thought about it, she felt a thrill of excitement which started in the pit of her stomach and ended up making her ears glow. She sometimes thought people would actually be able to see them glowing, if they were not hidden under her mop of hair. She smiled at the thought and Emma smiled too, with relief. The two girls got down from the table and went out together to play in the garden.

But that night, when her mother had kissed her 'Good night' and turned to

leave, Lou said suddenly, 'Lots of the
girls at the ballet class come from
Emma's new school . . . I've seen them
going in . . . in their uniforms. She'll
know them all . . . and I won't . . .
and then one of them will be her best

friend . . . and I'll be left out!' It was a wail of despair.

Her mother sat on the bed; she hugged Lou and wiped her eyes. 'Emma is your friend,' she said gently. 'She really likes you a lot and, after all, you do almost live together.'

Lou sniffled and snuffled.

'Trust me,' said her mother. 'It will be all right.'

Chapter Two

The changing room at the Maple School
of Ballet was packed with little girls
undressing. The bigger ones, like Lou
and Emma, had come straight from
school by themselves or had been
dropped off by parents in cars. The
smaller ones had been brought by
mothers or au pairs.

The younger ones were making a lot of
noise and confusion. Skirts were being

unbuttoned and jumpers pulled over heads and small bodies squeezed into stretchy, pale blue leotards. Hair was being brushed and pulled back into proper ballerina style. All this caused loud squeaks of protest and sometimes a howl of anguish as hasty hands pulled the wrong way.

The older girls were gathered in a group at one end of the room. They talked in lowered tones to make it quite clear that they were not part of the squeaking mass. Quite a few were hanging up the striped blazers and pleated skirts of Emma's school; others wore a uniform Lou did not recognize. None of them shared her flared grey skirt and the blue sweatshirt with the local school's logo. All the girls seemed to know each other, even those who came from different schools. Emma said, 'Hello!' eagerly to a girl who was in her class. The girl paused, in the middle of tying back long, blonde hair and said, 'Oh . . . hi!' in a bored voice. Then she looked away and began to talk to another girl.

Emma went pink and turned back to Lou. Lou tried not to feel pleased. She knew it was mean, but she was so afraid that Emma would become part of a group from which she would be left out. She gave Emma a big smile. Emma's pink face smiled back and faded to its usual colour.

Lou pulled up her tights, wriggled into her leotard and felt magic. She felt like a real ballet dancer. She longed to prance and leap about like the little ones, but she could see that it was not the thing if you were in the older class. The blonde girl had fixed her hair and was standing with her hands on her hips, her weight on one leg and the other toe slightly pointed. She looked like a dancer waiting in the wings of a theatre. Lou tried to imagine herself standing just like that, bored, unsmiling and very, very superior . . . but it was no use. She could only see herself madly leaping and twirling upon a brightly lit stage.

'Shall I do your hair?' asked Emma.

They had practised this over and over at home; Emma had learned how to do it at the ballet school's Beginners' Workshop. Lou scooped back her thick, dark hair and twisted it into a knot. Emma stuck in the hairpins to hold it in

109

place and fixed a little blue bun-net over it. Then Lou did the same for Emma's pale, smooth hair. This left only their shoes. Lou had hoped for satin shoes with ribbons that crisscrossed about the ankle, but the younger classes wore plain leather ballet shoes with bands of elastic. At least it made them easy to put on.

When they were ready, they looked up and found to their dismay that the older girls had disappeared.

'Quick!' said Lou. 'We don't want to turn up when the lesson has started!'

Panicking, they scrambled through the crowd and out into the quiet echoing hallway. They hurried across the polished floor to where voices came from a half-opened door. This led into a studio with mirror glass covering one wall and a wooden *barre* at which half a dozen girls stood doing *pliés* to warm up. The others were scattered about the room in various positions.

They turned as Lou and Emma came in and seemed surprised to see them. The blonde girl said something in a low voice and several of the others giggled.

Luckily, at that moment a tall, elegant woman swept into the room and said, 'Good afternoon, girls.'

An answering chorus said, 'Good afternoon, Mrs Dennison.'

'Find your spaces.'

The girls took up spaces around the room. Lou and Emma hid themselves at the back where the others wouldn't notice their efforts and snigger.

'*Révérence!*'

Twelve girls put the right foot forward, swept the left behind, raised their arms sideways and sank into an elegant curtsy with bowed heads; twelve girls rose smoothly again and stood in first position.

Lou and Emma did this beautifully as they had practised it with Mrs Dillon. Lou felt very pleased with herself. She began to wish that she had not hidden herself at the back.

Then the first blow fell. Mrs Dennison took out a list and began to call out names. The girls answered in turn, but Lou's and Emma's names were not included.

'The two girls at the back,' said Mrs Dennison, 'what are your names?'

'Lucy Lambert and Emma Browne,' said Lou.

'You are not on my list. What class are
you in?'

'I think we're in Beginners,' said
Emma, going pink again.

'Ah, Beginners are across the hall,' said
Mrs Dennison firmly.

Lou had never been so humiliated in all
her life. She went quite as pink as Emma

while a ripple of laughter spread around the room. They had to walk through all the others to reach the door and it seemed to take for ever. As she passed the blonde girl, Lou saw that she was trying to hide a cat-like smile.

When the door closed behind them and they stood alone in the empty corridor, Emma looked as if she might be going to cry.

'Oh, come on, Em, cheer up!' said Lou. 'Who wants to be with that snobby lot anyway?'

But there was worse to come. When Lou finally plucked up courage and opened the door across the hall, they found to their horror that it was full of the little ones!

Chapter Three

The studio had the same *barre* and mirrored wall, but the younger ones were not standing elegantly poised like the older girls. Some were hopping on one leg, others were squirming with nervousness. Several mothers sat on chairs at one side, smiling at the antics of their children.

I don't believe this! thought Lou. They cannot be serious. They can't expect Emma and me to dance with this lot!

Then she noticed a young, slim, sweet-faced woman who stood in front of the class, smiling at them expectantly. She had smooth, dark hair and wide eyes and reminded Lou of Margot Fonteyn dancing Juliet in her favourite video.

The young woman said, 'You must be Lucy and Emma. I am Miss Ashton and we are all very pleased to see you.' She turned to the class. 'Now, girls, we are very lucky to have Lucy and Emma with us for our first term. They are going to be at the front of the class and, as they already know a little about ballet, they will help to show you how the steps should be done.'

Lou suddenly felt much better. She

glanced at Emma and saw that she too
had brightened.

The teacher made room for them at the
front and as she did so she said, 'You'll
see that we have a little audience today.
Some parents like to stay for the first
lesson, to see that their daughters settle in
happily.' Then she turned to the whole
class and said, 'First we shall learn to do
a lovely curtsy, which is called a
révérence. I wonder if Lou or Emma can
tell me why we do this. Emma?'

'It's to greet the teacher and show
respect,' said Emma in a tiny voice.

'And to thank her for giving us
priceless knowledge,' added Lou, rather
more loudly. Mrs Dillon had told her that.

Miss Ashton smiled and said that they
were quite right. 'We do the *révérence* at

the beginning and end of every lesson,'
she told them. Then she swept into a
curtsy so graceful that Lou wondered why
she wasn't dancing on a grand stage
instead of teaching at the ballet school.

The lesson was under way and soon
Miss Ashton had the twelve younger ones

standing tall and raising their arms like birds' wings. Some got carried away and flapped a lot, so Miss Ashton asked Lou and Emma to demonstrate.

Lou began to see that there were good things about being in the Beginners' class. Instead of having to hide at the back and being the worst at everything, she and Emma were the best in the class. And Miss Ashton seemed to go out of her way to make them feel important. Lou even enjoyed the audience of mothers. She would have liked to have them there every week. She felt sure that they were all admiring her gracefulness and hoping that their daughters would learn to dance as well as she did. In fact, the mothers never took their eyes from their own little darlings and each one thought hers the star of the class, but fortunately Lou did not know this.

The lesson was very informal. After the little ones had all managed a rather wobbly *révérence*, they did a lot of moving to music. They flapped like birds, hopped like rabbits and danced like fairies. This was all a bit childish, and Miss Ashton had a particular smile for Lou and Emma which said plainly, 'Of course, all this is really too simple for you.' But it was great fun and Lou told herself that she was setting a standard for the others to aim at. Her bird flapped so lightly, it seemed as if it might take off at any moment. Her rabbit hopped so convincingly, you could have fed it lettuce. And as for her fairy . . . it was so graceful, she felt that she could certainly

have granted three wishes, if anyone had
bothered to ask for them.

After half an hour the younger ones
went to change, but Lou and Emma
stayed behind. Miss Ashton wanted to see
how much Mrs Dillon had taught them.
They did first, second and third foot
positions with the correct *port de bras*,

which were positions of the arms. They showed her their *pliés*, holding the *barre* lightly and bending their knees gracefully down and then up again. Lastly, they did *tendus*, which meant pointing their toes to the front, side and back.

All the steps in ballet seemed to have French names. Miss Ashton said it was because the first ballet school ever had been in France, hundreds of years before.

It was exciting to see themselves reflected in the great, clear wall mirror instead of the wardrobe door mirror that they used at home.

Miss Ashton said that they were doing very well. 'I hope you don't mind spending your first term with the Beginners,' she said, 'but we thought it would be best.'

'The older ones will make fun of us,' said Emma, who knew she would have to face them at school.

'But I think it would have been worse to make mistakes in front of them,' said Miss Ashton. 'You see, they have all been dancing for about two years. But with extra coaching, we hope you will be able to join their class next term. Miss Maple tells me that you are having special lessons from a lady who once danced with the great Bolshoi Company.'

'Yes,' said Emma proudly, 'she was called Reena Brushover.' (Her real name had been Irina Barashkova, but Lou and Emma were not good at Russian.)

'But she is Mrs Dillon now,' added Lou.

'Then I think that with such good

teaching you will soon catch up. Meanwhile –' she smiled at them – 'perhaps it would help if you finish a little early.'

Lou and Emma could have hugged her for understanding their problem. They were changed and dressed in a flash, and half-way home before the older girls came out.

Chapter Four

'There's this blonde girl called Angela who is really horrid to me,' said Emma gloomily.

Mrs Dillon clucked sympathetically. Lou's mother had gone to her evening class, Charlie was fast asleep and the girls had just finished their ballet lesson. It was fun being taught by Mrs Dillon, but she was very strict. They had done four positions with *port de bras* and they had

to get them just right. Then they did *pliés*
and *tendus* and something new called
glissés, which were like *tendus* only you
lifted your toes off the ground. Mrs
Dillon said they had worked very hard.

Now they sat drinking milk and eating
biscuits and told Mrs Dillon all their
troubles.

'This Angela is calling you rude names?' she asked.

'Well, no . . . But whenever I walk past her and her friends at school, I always hear them giggle.' Emma squirmed at the memory.

'Pouff! This is nothing!' said Mrs Dillon. 'With some girls there is always much giggling. Now when I first joined the Bolshoi school, I had to face real insults!'

'Did you?' Emma perked up. She loved to hear Mrs Dillon talk of the days when she had been Reena Brushover.

'Mostly they were city girls,' Mrs Dillon explained, 'while I was a little country girl, from beyond the mountains, who loved to dance. My accent was different from theirs and so they taunted me, calling me "peasant".'

'Oh, wow!' said Emma. 'You were like Giselle in the ballet. She was a peasant girl who loved to dance.'

Mrs Dillon thought about this and then preened, looking very pleased with herself. 'Yes,' she said, 'I was very much like Giselle.'

Lou had always wanted to know why Mrs Dillon had left the Bolshoi. Her mother said it was for love, but she had never dared to ask. Now she said casually, 'Did you fall in love with a nobleman . . . like Giselle?' She could picture him arriving in a carriage at the stage door and sending Reena Brushover baskets of flowers.

Mrs Dillon gave a dry little laugh. 'Alas, no,' she said. 'He was young man who moved the scenery.' She thought about him with a faraway look in her eyes and added, 'But he was very handsome.'

Lou wondered where he was now. 'Did he die?' she asked, thinking of her own father.

'No,' said Mrs Dillon, in a matter-of-fact voice. 'He was running away with an actress.'

'How awful!' said Emma. 'Did you go mad? . . . Like Giselle, I mean, when Loys deceived her.'

This time Mrs Dillon laughed out loud. 'I was very cross,' she said, 'but I did not go mad. I was very happy to be in England, even without my husband.'

'Were you dancing in England?' asked Lou.

'No, I did not dance after I left the

Bolshoi . . . but I gave lessons
sometimes.'

'Why didn't you join the Royal
Ballet?' said Emma.

'I tell you the truth,' said Mrs Dillon,
lowering her voice confidentially. 'For
some time, while I danced with the
Bolshoi, I was having pain in my knee.
Soon it would show, and I would have to
leave the company. I knew I would never
travel abroad again and life in Russia was
hard. I saw my chance with this
handsome young man. Once I was
married, no one could make me leave
England . . . not even when he left me.'

'But didn't your heart break when he
went?' asked Emma. 'Giselle's heart
stopped beating.'

'Her heart was weak,' said Mrs Dillon

scornfully. 'She was French, I think. But
the heart of a Russian peasant is strong;
she can bear much suffering.'

'Just as well,' said Lou practically, 'or
you could have ended up drifting around
the forest in a long white dress.'

'Like Giselle!' added Emma.

'This is true.' Mrs Dillon nodded
agreement. 'And you also must be

strong,' she told Emma. 'You must not let this giggling girl cause you pain. You will work hard at your dancing and then she will be the foolish one.'

Emma looked quite cheerful. 'Yes,' she said. 'I will . . . I'll work really hard . . . and then no one will be able to laugh at me.'

'WE'LL BE THE BEST,' chanted Lou. She punched the air and shouted, 'Yes!'

'Yes!' echoed Emma, following suit.

'You girls wake up Charlie,' growled Mrs Dillon, 'and I show you what real trouble is!'

Chapter Five

Lou and Emma were doing well. They were nearly half-way through the term and Miss Ashton said she felt sure they would be ready to move to the older class after Christmas. She also said that she would miss them, that it was a great help having them in the Beginners' class.

Lou and Emma loved Miss Ashton. Sometimes they felt they did not want to leave her class and join Mrs Dennison's.

Whenever they thought about it, they remembered that long, shameful walk to the door when she had thrown them out without a second thought. Miss Ashton, they agreed, would never have done that. She always went out of her way to make her pupils feel good. When Lou and Emma did their 'thank you' curtsy to her, they really meant it.

They were both very popular with the younger ones. Miss Ashton was very kind to her Beginners and Lou and Emma were trying to be just like her. So they never behaved as if they thought they were better than the others, but cheerfully joined in with all the skipping and hopping and flying about. Sometimes it was more like acting than dancing. Miss Ashton showed them how ballet dancers speak without words. For 'listen' you put one hand to your ear, for 'love' you clasped two hands to your heart and for 'marriage' you pointed to your ring finger.

The classes were great fun and afterwards the younger ones would crowd around them, saying, 'Lou, did you see

my rabbit jumps?' or 'Emma, is this how
a bird goes?'

As they entered the changing room
before their next lesson, the warm
welcome from the younger ones helped to
make up for Angela and her friends being
so snooty. The mothers and au pairs had
also become very friendly, saying, 'We
hear about "Lou and Emma" all the time,
when we get them home.' But today
Angela seemed to be speaking in an extra
loud voice and Lou knew that she meant
them to hear. 'I'm sure it will be *Aladdin*
this year,' she was saying, 'and they'll
need really graceful dancers in veils and
things.'

'Oh, you are sure to be chosen,' said
one of her friends and all the others
agreed.

Horrid little creeps! thought Lou crossly, and wondered what they were talking about. She tried to pretend she hadn't heard them, and she and Emma walked off to their class with heads held high, their hands clutched by the chattering little ones.

Miss Ashton's class followed the usual pattern until they came to the last five minutes, when she announced that she had some special good news for them.

'Every Christmas', she said, 'the local dramatic society puts on a pantomime. Do you all know what a pantomime is?'

'*Cinderella*, Miss!' . . . '*Beauty and the Beast*!' . . . '*Jack and the Beanstalk*!'

It seemed that everyone knew and had been to see more than one.

'That's good . . . good . . .' Miss Ashton

hushed them all. 'The ballet school chooses dancers to take part in the show. In the past it has always been girls from the older classes, but this year, because we have Lou and Emma to help us, we have decided to let the Beginners have a turn.'

The class went wild with excitement, and Lou and Emma looked at each other with broad grins. Angela would be furious, thought Lou with real glee. She pictured herself and Emma dancing gracefully in the 'veils and things', but what would the little ones wear? They would look a bit funny in veils.

'Please, Miss Ashton, which pantomime is it?'

'Guess,' said Miss Ashton.

They guessed in turn, but each time she

shook her head. Lou thought she knew and at last called out '*Aladdin*!' But Miss Ashton shook her head again.

'Give up!' chorused the young ones.

'It's . . . *Dick Whittington and His Cat* and you are all going to be . . . the little mice. Except for Lou and Emma, that is, and they are going to be TWO BIG RATS!'

As the two girls walked home together, Lou sighed. 'Veils and things would have been nice.'

'Yes . . .' said Emma doubtfully. She couldn't picture herself in veils. 'But rats and mice will be more fun,' she pointed out. 'I mean, it will be like being in *The Nutcracker*.'

Lou hadn't thought of that. Suddenly

the rats came to life in her mind. She
knew that she would be the most rat-like
rat ever. She grinned at Emma.

'Angela and her friends are all cats,'
she said, 'but we are the rats and –' she
raised her voice – 'RATS RULE! OK?'

'OK!' shouted Emma.

They raised their hands and slapped them together. Then they ran the rest of the way home, laughing.

Chapter Six

It was Emma's birthday the next week, but she wasn't happy.

'What can I do?' she asked Lou. 'Honestly, I wish I didn't have to have a birthday.'

Lou was shocked. She couldn't imagine anyone not wanting their birthday, especially if they had rich parents like Emma's who could buy her any present she asked for.

'Can't you tell your mum you don't want a party?' she asked. Lou always went to her own mother when things went wrong, and Mrs Browne seemed a very kind person.

'What? Tell her I don't want one because I haven't got any friends?' said Emma bitterly. 'Tell her that Angela shuts me out at school and the other girls do what she says?'

'Well, that's not your fault,' said Lou reasonably. 'I'm sure your mum would understand.'

'No, she wouldn't,' said Emma. 'She was always very popular at school. Everyone wanted to be her friend. She thinks because I'm her daughter I ought to be the same.'

There was a long silence.

'I've got friends at my school,' said Lou, trying to be helpful. 'We could invite them and then they could be your friends too.'

'But my mum would know they were from your school, wouldn't she?'

'I suppose so.' Lou could see no practical way to kit out her school friends in striped blazers for the day. Most of her friends wouldn't be seen dead in striped blazers anyway. There was another long silence. Then Lou had a brainwave.

'Couldn't you talk to my mum about it?'

Emma brightened at once.

They were minding Charlie, so they picked him up and lugged him downstairs to where Lou's mum was wrestling with her evening-class homework.

'Can we talk to you?' asked Lou.

Her mother looked up at the two solemn faces.

'Is it urgent?' she asked. 'Because I'm pretty busy.'

'It's urgent,' said Lou.

Jenny sighed and put down her pen. 'Well, I could use a break,' she said. 'Come and talk to me while I make some coffee.'

They crowded into the tiny kitchen.

Emma sat on the stool clutching Charlie, while Lou told her mother everything. Jenny listened seriously and thought hard while she poured milk and coffee. Then she said, 'Sometimes, when children get a bit old for party games and paper hats, they have birthday outings instead to somewhere exciting. Of course, they can't take lots of friends, because it would cost too much, so they just take their best friends.'

Emma gazed up at her with admiration. 'Oh, brilliant!' she said. 'So I could ask for an outing with Lou instead of a party and my mum would never know . . .'

'We could go to the ballet,' said Lou hopefully.

'Oh, yes!' From the depths of despair, Emma was suddenly on top of the world.

'I could say I wanted to see *The Nutcracker* . . . with the mice and rats. Oh, thanks, Mrs Lambert!' She dumped Charlie on the floor and gave Jenny a sudden hug, spilling her coffee. 'Let's go and ask now,' she said to Lou.

Charlie, who quite liked an adventurous life, shrieked joyfully as he found himself flying upstairs again, clutched between Lou and Emma. Mrs Browne was in her bedroom, winding heated rollers into her hair.

'Can we talk to you?' asked Emma breathlessly.

'Well, yes,' said Mrs Browne cautiously. 'As long as you keep Charlie away from the rollers.'

So Lou sat on the bed and played 'To market, to market, to buy a fat pig' with Charlie, while Emma told her mother her plans for the outing.

'I want to go to the Opera House and see *The Nutcracker*,' she said, 'and sit in the most expensive seats.' She thought this would make sure that she could only take Lou with her.

Mrs Browne seemed to like the idea. 'I suppose you are getting a bit old for party games,' she said, 'and you could wear your Laura Ashley dress, the one with the pink sash.' She seemed to be doing sums in her head as she unwound the rollers. 'I think', she said at last, 'that we could manage a party of five: you and me, and Lou, of course, and two of your other friends.'

Emma's face fell, but she thought fast. Then she asked, 'Can I have anyone I choose?'

'Of course,' said Mrs Browne. 'After all, it is your birthday.'

'Right,' said Emma triumphantly. 'Well, in that case I choose you and Lou, Lou's mum and Mrs Dillon!'

Chapter Seven

They had practised the dances over and over again. The first one came near the beginning of the pantomime. Dick Whittington had come to London to seek his fortune and was offered a job by a rich merchant if his cat could get rid of a plague of mice. The merchant had a beautiful daughter whom Dick fell in love with.

To their delight, the Beginners found

that this part would be played by Miss
Ashton. The merchant's daughter was
very frightened of mice, so they had to
chase her about and Miss Ashton had to
pretend to be scared. The little ones
thought it was great fun. They had to
hunch their shoulders and take tiny,
quick, mouse-like steps. They also had to

steal food from the tables and the cupboards. Then when the cat came, they dropped the food and ran away squeaking, while the merchant's daughter fainted gracefully into Dick Whittingon's arms.

Dick was played by a pretty young woman named Alison. She came to the ballet school to rehearse with them and strode about in tights, slapping her thighs. This was supposed to show that she was a boy. Lou thought it a bit odd, because none of the boys she knew ever strode about slapping their thighs. They were more inclined to slouch about and slap each other. Lou and Emma knew that the principal boys in pantomimes were always played by women and the dames by men, but no one seemed to know why.

The mice had an even better time in the second act. Dick and his cat had sailed with one of the merchant's ships to Africa, where the king had a serious rat and mouse problem. He offered Dick a fortune in gold if his cat could get rid of them. This fortune meant that Dick could marry the merchant's daughter, so of course the cat set to work and killed them all.

The children loved this, as they had to roll over and play dead with their legs stuck up in the air. The dead mice could be heard giggling as they were dragged off stage. The two rats, Lou and Emma, were the last to die. Lou did a very good stagger all over the stage before falling on her back. This made Alison laugh so much, she told Lou to keep it in.

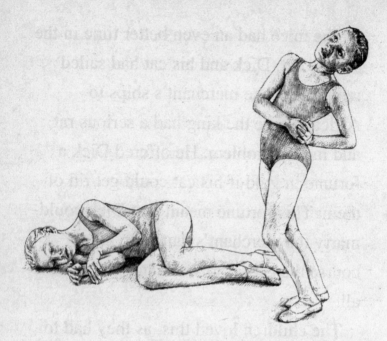

At last, the great day came when the dancers joined the rest of the cast for a rehearsal. Now they found themselves in a hall with a real stage, facing rows of empty seats. When Lou thought of the audience sitting in those seats, she got butterflies in her stomach.

The producer was called Adrian. He

flapped his hands about and called everybody 'darling'. He liked the dances Miss Ashton had arranged for her mice and laughed when Lou did her 'dying rat' for him. A stout older man, who was playing the Merchant, said something about 'children and animals, they'll act you off the stage if you give them half a chance', which raised a big laugh from the rest of the cast. Adrian told Lou to take no notice, as they were just jealous. Lou didn't mind anyway. It was so exciting to have an audience, even if it was only the rest of the cast. She didn't mind whether they clapped or laughed, so long as she made them do it.

When they had finished their dances, they sat in the seats and watched the others. Emma confessed to Lou that she found dancing for an audience rather scary, but Lou would not have it.

'Look,' she told Emma firmly, 'you once said your life was boring and I said it wouldn't be if you were my best friend. Right?'

'Yes,' said Emma doubtfully.

'Well, then,' said Lou. 'It's not scary, it's exciting! It's the same sort of feeling, Em, only it's good, not bad.'

'Oh,' said Emma, 'yes . . . I see . . .' She felt a lot better now that Lou had explained it.

The rehearsal went pretty well, although even the grown-ups got things wrong at times. Then Adrian would say, 'No, darlings . . . no. It's not working, is it? Let's have a little think.' Then he would change it, so that it worked better.

The Cat was played by a boy called Richard. He was Alison's brother and he was only fourteen. Lou liked him, but he wouldn't sit with her and Emma. She thought he was afraid of being lumped with 'the children'.

At the end of the rehearsal Adrian said, 'Well, it's coming along nicely, but we could do with a bit more business. Rack your brains, darlings, and see what you can come up with.'

'What's "business"?' Emma asked Miss Ashton as they went home.

'Well, it means little bits of action that add to the excitement or make the audience laugh,' she explained.

Lou thought this sounded very promising. She decided to dream up a bit more 'business' for the rats.

Chapter Eight

Mrs Browne had ordered a taxi to take them all to the door of the Opera House, so that they could arrive fresh and beautiful. The taxi had two extra little seats that folded down. Lou and Emma sat on these, facing the two mothers and Mrs Dillon. The old lady was wearing what Lou called her 'Reena Brushover outfit' and looked every inch the retired ballerina.

Lou and Emma were also looking the part. Emma had a white party frock with a full skirt and a pink sash. Normally Lou would have thought it too old-fashioned, but it seemed just right for going to the ballet. She had told her mother about it, and they went down to the charity shop and found another very similar one. Lou's was also white but it had smart pink bands on the bodice and around the hem.

The traffic was getting slower as they reached the centre of the city. Lou began to worry in case they were late, but at last the taxi drew up outside a big building with pillars and arches.

'Jump out,' said Mrs Browne. 'We're holding up the traffic.'

'Why is it called the Opera House if it's for ballet?' asked Emma.

Lou's mother explained that it was used for opera as well as ballet because both needed a very big stage.

Inside it was all red and gold. They left their coats in the cloakroom and made their way up a very splendid, red-carpeted staircase. Half-way up was a landing with a huge mirror reflecting the elegant visitors as they climbed the stairs. There was a long red-velvet bench in front of the mirror and Lou wished that she could sit on it.

At the top of the staircase, they showed their tickets to a young lady who directed them along a narrow corridor. Mrs Browne checked the number on her ticket with a row of numbered doors and said, 'This must be it.'

When they passed through the door,

Lou and Emma could hardly believe their
eyes. They seemed to be in a small red
and gold room with just five gold chairs
in it. But one wall of the room was
missing; instead you could look down
from a balcony into the whole vast
theatre.

'Where are we?' asked Emma in
astonishment.

'It's called a box,' said Mrs Browne proudly, 'and it's a special treat because it's your birthday.'

Lou was staring at the great curtains that hid the stage. She knew that she had seen them before and realized, with a shock, that this was the theatre where Margot Fonteyn had danced in *Romeo and Juliet*. Those were the curtains she had seen on the video the day she first decided to learn ballet. It seemed to her that she had come to a place of pure magic, and when the curtains swept aside and *The Nutcracker* began, she knew that she was right.

The first act took place at a party with little girls wearing dresses just like their own. Lou longed to join them, to dance with them on that brightly lit stage. But she had learned enough ballet by now to know that, although their dancing looked simple, it was way beyond her level. Clara, the heroine, looked rather like Emma, with smooth, fair hair. She was given a present of a wooden nutcracker, shaped like a strange little man. After the party, she fell asleep and all the toys came to life.

When the interval came, the two mothers went off to get a drink, but the girls did not want to leave the wonderful little box. So they stayed with Mrs Dillon and ate ice cream and admired the great auditorium and watched the audience come and go. There were lots of the little boxes on both sides of the theatre and quite a few had families with children in them. They stared at each other and some

163

little children on the other side waved. Lou and Emma waved back.

'I'd like to rent this box,' said Lou with a sigh, 'and live in it for the rest of my life.'

Emma said she would live with her.

In the second act, the strange Nutcracker and the toy soldiers fought against a horde of mice led by the evil King Rat. It ended in a sword fight which made Lou think about *Dick Whittington and His Cat* and the rats. The Nutcracker turned into a handsome prince and carried Clara away to the Land of Sweets. It ended with a wonderful display of glittering costumes and brilliant dancing.

At last it was all over. Lou and Emma were so dazzled that they could not bear to leave the little box.

'Can't we stay here and watch until the last person has gone?' begged Emma hopefully.

'We need to get our coats,' said Mrs Browne, 'and there will be a long queue.'

'We'll stay here with Mrs Dillon,' said Lou, 'and then meet you on that bench half-way up the stairs.'

The mothers agreed and the girls watched from the box as the big auditorium emptied. Then they made their way to the bench on the landing. Lou had set her heart on sitting there, knowing that everyone would look at them as they came down the stairs. One elderly woman smiled as she came towards them and then paused.

'May I just say how beautifully you all danced?' she said to Lou and Emma, in a

strong American accent. Before they
could answer, she turned to Mrs Dillon.
'Are you their teacher, ma'am?' she
asked.

'I am,' said Mrs Dillon politely.

'You must be very proud of them,' said
the American lady.

'Very proud,' said Mrs Dillon.

The lady smiled again and went on down the stairs.

Open-mouthed, the two girls stared after her. At last Emma said, 'She thought we were two of the dancers . . . from the ballet.'

'Yes,' said Mrs Dillon calmly.

'Because of our old-fashioned frocks?' added Lou.

'Yes,' said Mrs Dillon again.

'And you didn't tell her that we weren't,' said Emma wonderingly.

Mrs Dillon raised her eyebrows. 'Who am I', she said, 'to destroy a dream?'

Chapter Nine

The next rehearsal was a special one for the Rats and Mice. The costume designers were two students from the local art college and they had brought marvellous heads of papier mâché for the girls to try on. So far they had made only one of each, to see if they fitted well and could be worn comfortably during the dancing.

The mouse mask was rather sweet, but the rat mask looked wicked, and Lou and

Emma couldn't wait to try it on. At first it wobbled a bit, but Jo and Mike, the students, worked on it until it was quite steady. The eye-holes were a bit small, but a few snips with the scissors soon put that right.

'It's brilliant!' said Lou. 'It's as good as the ones in *The Nutcracker*.'

The students looked pleased, and it was true that when Lou wore it, she felt as if she was dancing on the stage of the Opera House.

She had watched the King Rat in *The Nutcracker* carefully. He had a wonderful way of twirling his whiskers, as if they were a big moustache. It made him look like a real villain. Lou tried it with the mask on and Adrian said it was 'a splendid bit of business'.

'Actually,' said Lou, 'I've got another bit of business from *The Nutcracker* –'

'What did I tell you?' interrupted the Merchant. 'Children and animals, they ought to be banned.'

'Shut up, Henry,' said Adrian, 'and let's

hear what she's got to say.'

'Well, you did ask us to dream up some bits,' said Lou indignantly.

'Take no notice of him,' said Adrian. 'He's just winding you up.'

The big man laughed and suddenly he reminded Lou of Jumbo Jones, her form teacher, who was often sarcastic but quite nice underneath. So she smiled at the Merchant and he smiled back.

'Come on, then,' said Adrian, 'let's have it.'

'Well,' said Lou, 'all the Mice and Rats getting caught . . . one after the other . . . it's a bit *samey*. But in the ballet, the King Rat and the Nutcracker fought with wooden swords . . . and I thought, maybe, Emma and I could fight with the Cat.'

'Yeah . . . great!' said Richard.

171

'Sounds good to me,' said Adrian. 'What about it, darling?' he turned to Miss Ashton. 'Could you arrange something? We don't want them hacking away at random and poking each other's eyes out.'

So, while the others rehearsed on stage, Miss Ashton took Richard and the two girls to the far end of the hall and they worked out the movements together.

Emma kept ducking every time Richard lunged towards her, so they agreed that the first Rat should die fairly quickly. Lou was to be a fiercer Rat and kept the Cat at bay for longer. Then, when he finally ran her through with his wooden sword, Lou did her long-drawn-out death stagger.

'My granddaughter will be sick as a parrot when she sees that.' It was the

Merchant's voice and Lou realized that he had been watching them. 'She wanted to be in the panto herself,' he added.

'Your granddaughter?' asked Emma.

'Yes,' said the Merchant. 'Name of Angela . . . Goes to your ballet class . . . Goes to your school too,' he said to Emma. 'Are you two friends?'

Emma looked embarrassed. 'Well, not really,' she said. 'I mean . . . I'm new this term . . . and she's already got friends.'

'Ah, like that, is it?' The Merchant nodded. 'Wants sorting out, that girl does. Bit of a madam at times.'

Their hearts warmed towards him.

As they went home, Emma said, 'Fancy him being Angela's grandfather! The Merchant, I mean. He's really nice, even if he does wind us up a bit.'

'Well, he would, wouldn't he?' said Lou. 'He's a Wind-up Merchant.'

Emma thought this was very witty and so did Lou. They tried it on Mrs Browne when they got home, but she didn't understand the joke. So they decided to save it for the next rehearsal and try it out on Richard.

Chapter Ten

Half the Mice were seriously over-excited and the other half were trembling in their ballet shoes. Lou and Emma, who were supposed to be keeping them in order, were too busy to be either scared or excited.

It was the day of the first performance. The set was in place, the lights had been tested and now, beyond the big closed curtains, the audience could be heard taking their seats.

Everyone backstage wanted to peep round the curtains, but Adrian said it would look 'unprofessional'. Lou agreed; no one at the Opera House had peeped. The red-velvet curtains had kept their secret right up to the wonderful moment

when they had swept back to reveal a complete and magical world. Now it was all about to happen again, she thought, only this time she would be on the other side of the curtain.

Meanwhile, it was her job to calm down half of her Mice and put courage into the others. 'You'll be all right,' she told them firmly. 'You won't see the audience because they're in the dark.'

'And if you do make a mistake, they won't know it's you,' added Emma helpfully, 'because you'll be inside your mouse masks.'

The Rats and Mice looked really convincing. They wore tights and leotards dyed brown and had long tails, which were a bit of a hazard when they were dancing. Sometimes tails got trodden on and there were squeaks of protest. Adrian said this was all right so long as they only squeaked and didn't call each other rude names. He said a bit of squabbling made them more mouse-like. They had been divided into two groups, one led by Lou and one by Emma. This had made it easier to give patterns to their dancing.

The assistant stage manager came round, calling, 'Overture and beginners, please.' This meant that the actors who were on stage first had to get ready in the wings. Lou wished she was one of them, so that she could get that first entrance over.

Miss Ashton came to wish them all good luck, but, as she had explained to them, you must not say 'good luck' in the theatre. Instead she said, 'Break a leg, all

of you!' And they chorused, 'Break a leg,
Miss Ashton!' in return.

Angela's grandfather came in to see
them, looking very splendid in his rich
costume. Lou's joke about the Wind-up
Merchant had gone all round the
company. Adrian said it fitted him

perfectly and even the Merchant seemed
to enjoy it.

'There are scouts from the Opera
House in the audience,' he said
breathlessly. 'It seems they have heard
about your Mouse troupe!'

They knew he was teasing, so they just
said, 'Yeah . . . yeah,' and told him to
break a leg.

One by one their friends vanished on
to the stage and then, at last, it was their
turn. The stage manager ushered them
into the wings; they glimpsed the dim
faces of the audience beyond the brightly
lit stage; their music began and they were
ON!

First they had to show what a nuisance
the Mice were by running about the stage
with little mouse-like steps, stealing food

from the Merchant's table. Each thing they stole had to be carried off-stage and dumped, so that they could run back on and steal something else. This made it look as if there were lots and lots of mice.

It worked very well for the little ones, as their first trip on to the stage was just a quick, scurrying dance and back into the safety of the wings. But it was like going on a scary ride at a fun-fair: when you had plucked up courage and done it once, you couldn't wait to do it again. Soon the little Mice had lost all their stage-fright and would probably have demolished the entire set, if Richard, the Cat, hadn't rushed in and chased them all away.

When the interval came, everyone was full of praise. Miss Ashton said she was proud of them and then gave Lou and

Richard a last-minute run-through of their sword fight.

The second act began. Now all the Mice were over-confident, and Lou and Emma had a job keeping them quiet backstage. It was a relief when it was time to go on. This scene was the Court of the African King, so they had all sorts of different food to steal. Sometimes two Mice grabbed the same piece and there were angry tussles. One of the Mice forgot to squeak and shouted, 'Let go! It's mine!' but this just raised a big laugh from beyond the footlights.

The audience was in a really good mood by the time it came to the sword fight. Emma's Rat had been killed and Lou found herself centre stage. For a while she and Richard circled each other,

clashing their wooden swords together.
Then the Cat lunged forward and there
was a gasp from the audience as he ran
the Rat through. Actually the sword thrust
went under Lou's arm, but it looked very
convincing and Lou began her death

stagger. She got rather carried away when she realized that every eye was upon her and the King Rat might have taken a very long time to die. Fortunately, she caught sight of Angela, watching from the middle of the front row. The shock of it finished her off and she fell to the floor. There was a sudden burst of applause from the audience and someone called out, 'Well done, that Rat!' Lying spread-eagled on her back, gazing up into the glare of the stage lights, Lou felt at that moment she could have died happy.

It was probably the best moment of all, but there were still good things to come. At the end of the show there were curtain calls and the Rats and Mice got some of the loudest applause of all. Coming on from the back of the stage, Lou and

Emma each led their little troupe of Mice
down to the footlights, where they spread
out, joined hands and did their best
révérences all together. The audience
cheered. Then, as Miss Ashton had taught
them, they removed their masks and,

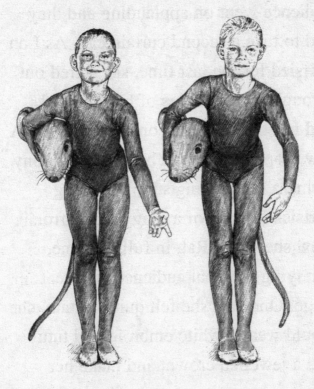

holding them in their hands, bowed so that the audience could see who they were. Then they put their masks back on and took their places at the side while the principal actors came on.

Even after the curtains closed, the audience went on applauding and they had to take a second curtain call. As Lou curtsied for the last time, she stared out through the eye-holes of her rat mask and felt that she had come a long way. A few months back, she had been a skinny girl in a red bathing suit, practising curtsies in front of a dingy old mirror. Now she was a Rat, in full costume, curtsying to a real audience on a real stage. One day, she felt quite certain, she would wear a white embroidered tutu and a jewelled crown, and make her graceful *révérence* in front of those magical red and gold curtains on the stage of the Opera House.

Antonia Barber

Dancing Shoes
Friends and Rivals

Illustrated by Biz Hull

Chapter One

Lou stood on the corner of the street waiting for Emma. She shivered and pulled her coat closer around her. There was a cold wind blowing which was making her nose red. The snow, so white and magical a week before, was now grey with city dirt. It was melting fast, clogging the gutters and making puddles across the pavements. Lou's feet were freezing. She wished she could hurry on

to the warm changing room but she had
promised to meet Emma on the corner
after school so that they could arrive at
the Maple School of Ballet together. It
was their first lesson in the new class and
it was not going to be easy.

The Brownes' estate car pulled up
sharply at the corner, showering icy water
over Lou's feet. The
door flew open and a
pink and flustered
Emma jumped out.

'I'm sorry, Lou, I
couldn't find my ballet

bag. Someone had put it on the wrong peg. Are we very late?'

Lou waved to Mrs Browne as the big car pulled away from the kerb. 'It's OK,' she said, 'but we'd better get a move on.'

'Will they give us a bad time?' asked Emma as they hurried along the street.

'Sure to,' said Lou gloomily. 'You know what Angela is like.'

Emma knew only too well. She went to school with Angela, who was the most powerful girl in her class. If you didn't belong to Angela's group you were nobody, and she chose to leave Emma out. Even Lou had no idea how lonely Emma was, though she knew that her friend was not happy. They both wished they could go to the same school, but the Brownes sent their daughter to a private school while Lou's mother sent her to the local primary.

'I wish we could stay on in Miss Ashton's ballet class,' said Emma wistfully.

'It was fun,' agreed Lou. They had both enjoyed their first term in the beginners' class, especially when they were chosen to take part in the local pantomime. 'But we've got to move on, Em, if we really want to be ballet dancers. We'll have to work hard to catch up with Angela and the others.'

Emma sighed.

They ran up the wide stone steps of the Maple School of Ballet and along the echoing hallway. At the door of the changing room they paused to get their courage up. As they did so, Lou sensed suddenly that something was different.

'Wait,' she said, catching at Emma's sleeve. 'Listen!'

The familiar sounds of the younger ones dressing and having their hair done had changed somehow. The usual squeaking had become a distinct giggling and the shrieks were more like little squeals of excitement.

'Something's up!' said Lou and she pushed open the door.

Inside the changing room it seemed that all eyes were being drawn towards the far end of the room.

'Oh!' said Lou.

'Oh, Lou!' said Emma.

In the corner with his back towards them, raising his arms to pull his sweatshirt over his head, was a BOY . . .

Lou and Emma knew perfectly well that there were men in ballets. They even knew, if they thought about it, that these dancers must have had lessons when they were young. But they had never seen a boy at the Maple School of Ballet and they could not imagine any of the boys they knew going to ballet classes. Boys played football; they slouched about in sloppy clothes. They did not pull on tights and do *pliés*! Any boy who did that would be the biggest wimp in the world . . .

But then the Boy turned round and he didn't look at all wimpish. He was tall but not too thin, with smiley eyes and dark curly hair. Lou and Emma stared like all the others.

The Boy made his way through the

crush with his head lowered as if to avoid looking at the girls. As he reached the doorway he looked up and caught Lou's eye. He raised one eyebrow and grinned ruefully. Before she could recover and grin back, he had gone, followed by Angela and her friends in a breathless excited rush.

'Quick!' said Lou. 'Or we'll be the last.' She could not bear to think of the Boy talking to the simpering Angela.

But when they reached the studio, they found all the girls posing elegantly, while the Boy chatted to the elderly pianist.

Mrs Dennison followed them in and the class began. She put the three newcomers at the back, which gave Lou a chance to return the Boy's grin. She wondered if he would speak to her at the end of the class, but Mrs Dennison asked him to stay behind. She said Miss Maple wanted to see him. In the changing room the girls talked of nothing else.

'We needn't have worried,' said Emma as they walked home. 'I mean, Angela and her friends didn't make fun of us at all.'

Lou laughed. 'They didn't even notice *us*,' she said. 'That boy came in really useful.'

'He was nice, wasn't he?' said Emma.

'He wasn't just *nice*,' said Lou. 'He was . . . he was . . .' She couldn't find the right word to describe him. Then, shivering in the cold wind, she said at last, 'He was really special!'

Chapter Two

Melanie Jackson summed it up for the girls at the local junior school. 'He is *so* cool!' she said with the air of one who knew about these things.

'Nice face,' said Liza Tompkins.

'And clever with it!' said Tracey Gibbs.

Lucy listened but said nothing. She had not yet recovered from the shock of finding that the Boy actually went to her school.

'I bet he does gymnastics,' said Melanie. 'You can tell by the way he moves.'

'You only hope!' said Liza. 'Just because you do gym.'

'He does ballet,' said Lou, finding her voice for the first time.

'Ballet!'

'Boys don't do ballet!'

'You're joking!'

'Rudolf Nureyev did.'

'That's different. I mean boys from *our* school don't.'

'Well, this one does,' said Lou, 'because he goes to my ballet class . . . and he's pretty good too.'

Now she was the centre of attention.

'Does he wear tights?' (*giggle, giggle*)

'Did you talk to him?'

'What did he say?'

Lou did not want to admit that she had not spoken to him so she said, 'Oh, you know, this and that.'

She could see that her popularity had risen by several notches.

Walking home from school, they saw the Boy behind them, one of a group on bicycles, weaving lazily along the edge of the kerb. The girls raised their voices and kept looking round . . . Lou found it rather embarrassing. She had the longest walk home, and one by one her friends went their separate ways. When she was alone, she did look back and saw the Boy a little way behind. He caught her up, got off his bike and said, 'Hi! It's Lucy, isn't it?'

'Lou.' Her mouth went dry.

'I'm Jerome . . . after the songwriter, not the saint. My friends call me Jem.'

'Why were you named after a songwriter?'

'Because my gran is a Jerome Kern fan.'

'Who's he?' asked Lou.

'Oh, some famous songwriter. My gran also likes one called Cole Porter and another called Irving Berlin, so it could have been worse.'

'Your friends would have called you "Irv",' said Lou. They both made sick noises.

'Or Old King Cole?' he suggested.

'Even worse,' said Lou.

There was a silence while she tried to think of something sparkling to say. As they turned into her street a cold wind whipped them so she said, 'My mum makes hot chocolate when I get in. Would you like some?'

'Oh, great!' said Jem.

Lou had never brought a boy home before. He chained his bike to the railings while she opened the door. 'Hi, Mum!' she called. 'Hello, Soggybottom!'

'Not 'Bottom!' said Charlie indignantly, hugging her knee.

'Well, "Hi, Charlie" then.' Lou picked him up. 'My brother,' she explained to Jem and, as Jenny came out of the kitchen, she added, 'My mum.' To Jenny she said, 'This is Jem. He's new at school and he goes to our ballet class.' She wished she and Emma had not raved on about him so much the night before.

Jenny Lambert grinned. 'Brave lad!' she said. 'How do you cope with all those girls?'

'The changing room was a bit much,' said Jem, 'but Miss Maple says I can use the staff room.'

'Do the boys at school tease you?'

'They haven't found out yet. But I suppose they will . . . They did at my other school.'

'Did you mind?' asked Lou.

Jem shrugged. 'It was a pain,' he said, 'but I play a lot of football, so they decided I was OK.'

'Are you going to be a dancer?' asked

Lou. She had already altered her dream future to include him: a tall, curly-haired Nureyev standing by her side while she took her curtain calls.

'Don't really know. But I want to go to stage school and my gran says I'll need ballet to get in. My grandad is teaching me piano too.'

Lou wavered; maybe she would go to stage school too, instead of ballet school. But her dream of one day wearing a white-embroidered tutu was strong . . . and there was plenty of time to make Jem change his mind.

The door to the upstairs flat slammed and Emma came clattering down the stairs. She burst into the kitchen and stopped dead at the sight of Lou and Jem, side by side, drinking hot chocolate.

'Oh!' she said and turned rather pale.

'Hi!' said Lou. 'It's Jem . . . from the ballet class.'

'Yes,' said Emma. 'I can see.'

She did not look very happy; Lou thought maybe she was a bit jealous.

Jenny made some more hot chocolate.

'You're Emma, aren't you?' said Jem.

'Yes,' said Emma, brightening.

'You go to the same school as that Angela?'

'Yes,' said Emma darkening.

'Wow! What a girl!'

He realized suddenly that the warm kitchen had grown very frosty. Both girls were looking daggers at him and Lou's mum was making warning signals above their heads.

'Good ballet dancer, I mean,' he said hastily. 'Long legs . . . Dancers need long legs . . . I mean *strong* legs . . .'

They were still glaring at him.

He put down his mug and glanced at his watch. 'Gosh, is that the time?' he said. 'Well, I suppose I'd better be on my way . . . Thanks, Mrs Lambert . . .'

Chapter Three

Sometimes Lou felt cross with Jem and sometimes she felt cross with Emma. She knew this was not fair, but if Em had not come in when she did, Jem might never have mentioned Angela. And to make things worse, she did rather go on about it.

'I think he really likes Angela,' she would say.

'If he likes *her*, why did he walk home with me?'

'Well, Angela doesn't go to your school.'

'He could have walked with one of the other girls.'

'They don't go to the ballet class. Maybe he wanted to ask you about her . . .'

Lou was afraid she might be right, which made her even more cross.

The next night the boys had football practice and then it was the weekend. On Monday night Jem was nowhere to be seen. On Tuesday he rode behind Lou but did not try to catch up with her. She didn't look round. That night Lou had a serious talk with Emma.

'He'll be at ballet class tomorrow,' she said, 'and if we're horrid to him and

Angela is nice, he'll end up being her friend.'

'Well, yes . . . but . . .' Emma did not want to turn the twosome into a threesome. What if Lou became Jem's friend while she was left out? It was bad enough to have no friends at school, but if Jem took Lou away . . .

'Angela is vain enough now,' said Lou. 'If Jem is *her* friend she'll be impossible.'

'I suppose so . . .'

'And my mum says it's silly to be huffy just because he said . . .' Lou could not bring herself to repeat the offending words.

'Oh, well, in that case . . .' Emma thought very highly of Jenny Lambert's good sense.

*

Next evening in the changing room there was an air of deep gloom. The Boy was nowhere to be seen and all the little ones were moaning.

'It's all right,' Lou told them. 'He's changing in the staff room so he doesn't see all of you in your KNICKERS!'

The little ones giggled at the naughty word.

'How do *you* know?' asked one of Angela's friends.

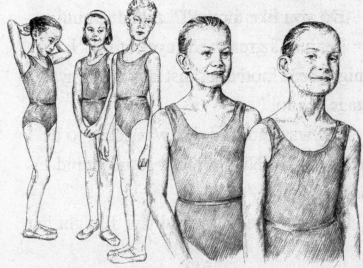

'He told me on the way home the other night,' said Lou cheerfully. 'Didn't you know? He goes to my school.'

She swept out of the changing room with Emma, trailing clouds of glory.

Jem was already in the studio.

'Hi!' said Lou brightly. 'Haven't seen you all week.'

He seemed pleased that he was no longer in the doghouse.

'I did a lot of football practice,' he said.

'Do you like football?' asked Emma.

'Yeah, it's great!' His eyes lit up. 'I might be a footballer instead of going to stage school.'

Lou was shocked. He was going to be her personal Nureyev, not some stupid footballer.

Emma looked at him shyly. 'I might be

a teacher,' she confided. Lou glared at her. Emma looked guilty. 'Of course, I'd rather be a ballet dancer,' she said quickly, 'but I'm not as good as you are, Lou.'

'You could be a ballet teacher,' said Jem, and Emma smiled at him gratefully.

Mrs Dennison arrived with the others and the class swept into their graceful *révérences*, all except Jem, who did an elegant bow.

Lou wanted to watch him, so she stood behind him at the *barre*. But Mrs Dennison promptly changed them around and left Lou knowing that he was watching her. She did all her exercises as beautifully as she could and Mrs Dennison said, 'Well done, Lucy.'

But Lou was now standing behind

Angela and she could not help seeing that the fair girl was very good indeed. Her legs *were* long and seemed made for ballet. Her arms never seemed to have elbows sticking out, her head was gracefully poised on a slender neck. Lou

did not like her at all. She was mean to Emma and much too pleased with herself. I must keep Jem out of her clutches, she thought. She won't really want him for a friend, she'll just want to show him off.

'You are sticking your bottom out, Lucy,' called Mrs Dennison. 'Do keep your mind on your dancing!'

Now Lou felt really foolish and it was all Angela's fault!

As they hurried to change at the end of the lesson, Lou wondered if Jem would follow them home. She felt sure that he would . . . But as they came out on to the steps, a cold rain was falling and Mrs Browne was waiting to take them home in the car.

Chapter Four

On Saturday it was almost like spring.
The wind dropped; the sun came out and
the street market was crowded. The stall-
holders breathed in the bright air and
greeted their customers with a smile.
Emma had abandoned her parents on
their trip to the supermarket to go with
Lucy and her mother. The girls were
taking turns with Charlie's pushchair.

Mrs Dillon, the old lady who lived on

the top floor of the Brownes' house, had also joined the shopping party. Since Jenny Lambert had introduced her to the delights of the charity shops, she had been slowly changing her entire wardrobe. Each week her clothes grew more exotic. Lou and Emma were quite proud of her.

Now they rummaged together through piles of brilliant colour on a stall selling silk scarves. Lou could see Mrs Dillon eyeing the elegantly tied headscarf of a tall good-looking woman who lifted the bright silks with a slender, long-fingered hand. The woman laughed, turning to speak to the boy beside her, and Lou saw with a start that it was Jem. He looked up and grinned. 'What do you think, Lou? My gran can't decide between this

orangy-yellow one and that yellowy-
orange.'

Lou couldn't see much difference but
Mrs Dillon said firmly, 'This orangy-
yellow is best. It is giving your lovely dark
skin a rich glow.'

'Well, thank you . . .' The woman gave

Mrs Dillon a slow, charming smile. Lou thought she had never seen anyone so beautiful. She looked much too young to be Jem's grandmother.

A moment later he asked, 'Is that your gran?'

'Mrs Dillon?' said Lou, taken by surprise. 'No, she lives upstairs in our house and she helps us with our ballet practice.'

'She used to dance with the Bolshoi,' put in Emma. 'She was called Reena Brushover.'

'The Bolshoi! Wow!' Jem looked again at the old lady. 'You can see she's been on the stage. She's got that sort of style.'

Lou thought of Mrs Dillon when they had first met her – the dowdy brown frock and the sagging cardigan – but she only said, 'Your gran looks amazing too. Was she on the stage?'

'Still is,' said Jem. 'She's a singer and my grandad plays the clarinet. They met when they did a gig together.'

Lou began to see why he wanted to go to stage school and why he was not afraid to be seen in a ballet class. She was wishing her own family were more glamorous when she felt Emma jogging her elbow. She was trying to point out something behind Jem's back. Glancing over his shoulder, Lou saw Angela with her grandfather, looking at Indian jewellery on the next stall. Angela caught her eye and turned away. But Lou knew that she had seen them talking with Jem and that she was not pleased.

'Why are you both grinning like that?'

asked Jem. 'You look like a couple of cats who have been at the cream.'

'Oh, it's nothing,' said Lou airily.

'Nothing at all,' said Emma.

The women had moved on to a stall selling tropical vegetables, and Jem's gran was explaining to Lou's mum and Mrs Dillon how to cook some of the more unusual ones.

'You must come to us one day,' she said, smiling. 'Bring all the children. We will cook a Caribbean meal and play music together.'

Lou looked at Emma; Emma looked at Lou. They had been invited to Jem's house! Angela would be green with envy.

And then, 'How are my favourite Rats?' said a booming voice beside them.

They looked up to see Angela's

221

grandfather smiling down at them, while Angela looked away and tried to pretend they were not there. Lou and Emma liked this fat, friendly man. They had met him when they took part in the local dramatic society's pantomime. He had played the Merchant in *Dick Whittington* and Lou and Emma had played the Rats. Lou had nicknamed him 'The

Wind-up Merchant' because he was always teasing them. The Rats grinned at him and said they were fine.

'You know my granddaughter Angela?' asked the Wind-up Merchant.

Lou and Emma said they did, but the girls did not speak to one another. The big man seemed disappointed.

'I hope you're both coming to Angela's party?' he said. 'Have you had your invitations?'

'Er . . . no . . .' said Lou.

Angela looked furious.

'They must be in the post,' said her grandfather. 'Saturday week . . . Mark it in your diaries.' And with that he moved on into the crowd, followed by Angela with her nose in the air.

'Was he winding us up again?' asked

Emma as they watched him go. 'I mean, Angela is never going to invite *us* to her party.'

'Maybe he was winding Angela up,' said Lou. 'You know what a tease he is!'

'What was all that about rats?' asked Jem, and they had to tell him about the pantomime.

'And will you go to her party . . . if you do get an invitation?' he asked.

Emma began to say, 'Well, if . . .' but Lou said firmly, 'She needn't worry. We wouldn't go to her rotten party if she paid us!'

'Ah, if only Angela would invite *me* to her party,' said Jem, rolling his eyes, 'I'd go like a shot!'

They both hit him.

Chapter Five

'Shoulders back, Emma. Raise your chin. You must stand tall and proud. A dancer must draw every eye towards her.' Mrs Dillon drew herself up and looked very superior. Emma tried to look the same.

'That is better. Do you not feel more confident?'

Emma sighed. People were always telling her to be more confident, so she tried to pretend that she was. She was not

even honest with Lou any more.
(*Arms into first position*
. . . look at hands
. . . left arm to second
position . . . look
right . . .) Lou
told her just
how to deal with
the girls at school
(*Right arm to*
second . . . look
over left arm . . .),
but when she got there, she couldn't do it.
And because she was ashamed of being
feeble, she pretended things were getting
better. (*Look to front . . . hands on waist . . .*)
But it wasn't true. (*Face front, third position,*
right foot in front . . .) If only Angela would
invite her to the party. (*Bend knees . . .*

226

demi plié . . . *three times . . .*) If just for
once, she could talk and laugh with the
other girls . . . (*Back to third, right foot
in front . . .*)

'Left foot, Emma,' said Mrs Dillon.
'Your mind is wandering.'

If they got to know her, they might
even like her . . . Lou liked her . . . Was
there an invitation in the post? If there
was, it would come tomorrow. But Lou
said that she wouldn't go even if she was
invited . . . and Emma knew that she
would never go without Lou.

At last Mrs Dillon said, 'That will do
now. You have been good girls. Now I go
and see if Charlie is still sleeping. Your
mother will be back from her evening
class soon.'

The girls did their *révérences* and then

flopped on to Emma's bed. They did their practice in Emma's room now because Mr Browne had fixed up a big mirror which he had found in a junk shop. It was a bit worn in places but it helped the girls to see their mistakes. He had also fitted a baby monitor so that Mrs Dillon could hear if Charlie woke up during their practice session.

There was a lot of noise and confusion in the Brownes' part of the house. Emma's father was refitting their kitchen.

'We'll have to watch on your video,' said Emma. 'Dad's drill makes our picture go all funny. It's like this every evening now. I wish he'd get a builder to do it while I'm at school.'

'Can't he get one?' asked Lou as they went downstairs. She thought Mr Browne must be able to afford a builder: he had an important job in a bank.

'He likes doing it,' Emma sighed. 'He says he'd rather be a carpenter than a banker.'

'So why doesn't he?'

'My granny wouldn't let him. She said she didn't pay a fortune for his schooling to have him be a carpenter.'

'Jesus was a carpenter,' Lou pointed out.

'That's what my dad said, but Granny said Jesus didn't have an expensive private education.'

Lou thought about it. Emma went to a private school. 'Will you have to be what your granny says?' she asked.

'I expect so,' said Emma gloomily.

'Will she let you be a ballet dancer?'

'Shouldn't think so. I expect I'll have to work in a bank too.'

'How awful!' said Lou.

Mrs Browne had managed to get them a videotape of *Petrushka*. It was about a puppet show. Petrushka was a clown who was in love with a little ballerina, only she was in love with a fierce Moor. The dancing was lovely but it was very sad and the little clown died in the end. Emma cried. She hated to see him so sad and lonely.

Mrs Dillon made a hot drink while Lou got out the biscuit tin. Mr Browne started hammering overhead, which woke up Charlie. He came out rubbing his eyes, climbed on to the sofa and settled down on Emma's lap. She cuddled him and they both seemed to be comforted.

'I have good news,' said Mrs Dillon
when he was asleep again. 'Miss Maple is
asking me to be a patron of the ballet
school.'

'What's a patron?' asked Lou.

'Well . . .' Mrs Dillon didn't seem quite sure herself. 'It seems I am to judge competitions and give special coaching for older girls who try for the Royal Ballet School.'

'Wow!' said Lou. 'You'll be really important!'

She wondered if Mrs Dillon would judge their class at the end-of-term display. And, if so, would it help that Mrs Dillon was her friend? Would she give her better marks than Angela?

'I have more news.' Mrs Dillon hesitated. 'Perhaps you are not liking this so much.'

'Tell us,' said Lou anxiously. Suppose Mrs Dillon was too busy being a patron now to take their practice?

'I am having coffee one morning with

Mrs Sinclair.'

Lou and Emma did not know anyone by that name.

'She is asking me if her grandson can join our practice . . . but perhaps you are not liking a boy in the class?'

'A boy,' said Emma doubtfully. 'What's his name?'

'Is Jeremy, I think,' said Mrs Dillon.

'No it's not,' said Lou with a wide grin. 'It's Jerome . . . after the songwriter, not the saint.'

Emma was no wiser.

'She means Jem!' said Lou. 'He's going to join our practice! Angela will just *die* when she finds out.' Her voice rose to a high pitch with excitement.

'You will die, if you wake Charlie again,' warned Mrs Dillon. 'Does this mean that you are liking this boy to come?'

'Oh, yes, *please*,' said Lou and Emma in chorus.

'Then I shall ask your mothers if they are approving.' Mrs Dillon picked up Charlie and carried him back to bed, leaving the two girls grinning on the sofa.

Chapter Six

The invitations came on the Wednesday morning. '*ANGELA*', they said, '*is having a PARTY.*' At the bottom of each, the Wind-up Merchant had scribbled, '*Please come! It wouldn't be the same without my Rats.*'

Emma came racing downstairs. She had been invited! At last she might make some friends at school . . . But suppose Lou refused to go?

'Have you got one?' she asked breathlessly.

Lou was very laid-back about it. 'Angela's party?' she said. 'Mmm . . . I suppose we'd better go, or the Wind-up Merchant might be hurt.'

'Oh, yes!' said Emma. 'That's what I thought. I mean . . . he *is* our friend and the party *is* at his house and I expect he planned it all.'

'And he does say it won't be the same without us,' said Lou. 'Yes, I think we'd better go.'

Actually, she wanted to go almost as much as Emma did. She was curious to see where Angela lived; she knew that it was one of the big houses near the park. And she knew that if they were not there, they would have to spend weeks in the

changing room, listening to all Angela's
friends going on about how
WONDERFUL it had been.

Emma set off to school in high spirits
. . . but she came home in tears.

'Angela was really horrible to me when
I tried to thank her for the invitation,' she

sobbed in Lou's room. 'She turned to her friends and said that it was her grandfather who'd invited me (*sob, sob*) and that *she* would be too proud to go to a party (*snuffle, snuffle*) if she hadn't been invited (*sniff, sniff*) by the person whose birthday it was (*sob*), and then all her friends looked at me as if I was rubbish.'

Lou hugged her, and Charlie, who hated to see anyone crying, gave her some of his rather messy kisses. 'That girl is the *pits*,' said Lou. 'Just wait till I see her at ballet class!'

'I don't think I'll go tonight,' said Emma, blowing her nose. 'I'll tell my mum I've got a headache . . . Well, I have anyway.'

Lou did not try to change her mind. She thought it would be better if Emma

was not there. Emma did not like to see
people quarrel.

Lou went storming into the changing
room with a face like thunder.

'You', she said to Angela, 'are a mean-
minded little PIG . . . No, you're not,
because pigs are nicer than you . . . You
are a rotten BULLY. You pick on Emma
because she's shy and kind and you know
she won't hit back.'

A terrible silence had fallen over the
room. The young ones clutched at their
mothers and gazed at Lou with open
mouths. One mother snatched up her
little darling and covered her ears. Angela
flushed bright red and her friends stared
at Lou in horror.

'And if you think Emma and me want

to come to your stupid party, you're wrong!' shouted Lou. 'We wouldn't be seen *dead* at it.' She held out the invitations, tore them into shreds and threw the scraps in a heap at Angela's feet. Then she stormed out again.

Once in the quiet corridor, she could hear her heart beating. She dived into the studio where she found Jem on his own,

idly tinkling at the piano. He took one look at her face and said, 'Wow! What happened?'

'Don't ask!' shouted Lou, who had just realized that she had not changed yet. She could not go back. 'Just play the piano,' she said, 'and don't turn round. I have to get my things on.'

Everything went wrong. She got her tights in a twist and her leotard on backwards.

Jem listened to her little cries of despair and said, 'Do you want some help?' His voice was full of laughter.

'No, I don't!' she yelled. 'And don't turn round!' She was back to her knickers and getting desperate. The others would come in at any moment and she would look such a FOOL!

At last she got it right and said, 'OK, you can turn round now.'

Jem looked her up and down. 'Hmm,' he said, 'I don't think Mrs Dennison will be keen on that hairstyle.'

Lou clutched at her hair, which she had quite forgotten. She and Emma usually did each other's. Frantically she wound it about, but her fingers had all turned into thumbs. Each time, one lock of hair fell out at the last moment.

'Come here, I'll have a go,' said Jem calmly, when she was almost in tears. He sat her on the piano stool, wound her hair into a neat bun and snapped the little blue bun-net over it. He was just sticking in her hairpins when the door opened and Angela and the others came in . . .

*

'It was brilliant,' Lou told Emma when she got home. 'You should have seen the look on her face! I think she minded more when she saw Jem fixing my hair than she did when I yelled at her.'

But she did not tell Emma about her talk with Jem on the way home. He had wanted to know what it was all about, and Lou had jumped at the chance to tell him what Angela was really like, pouring out the whole story of the bullying and Emma's tears . . . And now she felt really guilty. What Emma had told her was private; she was not supposed to tell anyone else. And Lou had no excuse. After all, it wasn't as if Jem could *do* anything about it.

Chapter Seven

On Friday morning a letter arrived for Emma. It said:

> Dear Emma
> Please come to my birthday party. I would really like you to come. I am sorry if I was mean to you. Please make Lucy come too.
> From Angela

Emma could hardly believe it. She raced

downstairs and met Lou on her way up. Lou read from the note she held in her hand:

> Dear Lucy
> Please come to my birthday party. I would really like you to come. I am sorry if I was mean to Emma. Please make her come too.
> From Angela

'What is she up to now?' she said. 'Her grandfather must have made her write these.'

'Do you think so?' asked Emma. She had been hoping that Lou's telling-off had suddenly changed Angela into a really nice person. 'I suppose you're right,' she sighed. 'So, do you think we should go?'

'Let's see how she treats you at school today,' said Lou wisely.

When Emma got home, Lou was waiting.

'Was she nice to you?'

'Well . . . yes . . .' said Emma,

'only . . . she was sort of *too* nice . . . I mean, as if she was *acting* a nice person.'

Lou snorted. 'She's up to something,' she said. 'Maybe the Wind-up Merchant said he would cancel the party if we didn't come.'

'Why would he do that?' asked Emma. 'She's his granddaughter and he's bound to be fond of her.'

'True . . .' said Lou. 'It does seem a bit odd. Maybe he's winding *her* up. Maybe he *said* he would stop the party . . . but he wouldn't really.'

'It *was* better at school,' said Emma wistfully. 'I mean . . . her friends were nicer to me. They asked me to sit at their table at lunchtime.' And yet she remembered how uncomfortable she had felt . . . the pretend politeness, the secret smiles. It was better than being ignored, but not *much* better.

It was Jenny Lambert's evening class that night, when Mrs Dillon came to babysit Charlie and gave them their practice session.

They were working hard to catch up with the rest of the class, so that they could do their first grade exam at the end of the year. Each week Mrs Dennison wrote in a little notebook the steps they were to practise, and Mrs Dillon made sure that they did them properly.

And now Jem was to join them.

'We will have no nonsense because this boy is coming,' warned Mrs Dillon. 'We will not have gigglies or showing off.'

Lou and Emma were shocked.

'Gigglies!' they protested. 'Showing off! Of course we won't!' And they both giggled.

'Do your giggling before the boy comes,' advised Mrs Dillon. 'Once he is here, we will have discipline!'

When Jem arrived she was very stern, which made him strangely shy and a bit nervous. Lou and Emma saw that he treated the old lady with great respect, listening carefully when she corrected his movements. This made them behave themselves and take the practice session very seriously. It was, as Lou said afterwards, 'all a bit heavy' until Charlie woke up.

As the ballet practice neared its end, they suddenly heard him, banging on his cot and calling, 'Lou! . . . Lou! . . .

Bottom want Lou!'

This made it impossible not to giggle. Even Mrs Dillon laughed. 'We will have your *révérences* now,' she said, 'and then we will be seeing what that young man is up to.'

As Lou curtsied, with Jem bowing beside her, she pretended that they were on the stage at the Opera House. She imagined how he would one day take her hand and present her to the audience, making it clear that she was the real star. The audience would shout for her, 'Lou! Lou!'

Jem waved his fingers in front of her eyes. The vision faded; she was back in Emma's bedroom and Charlie was beginning to wail.

They did not watch a video that night, but Jem stayed for a drink and talked to Mrs Dillon about the days when she had been Irina Barashkova and danced with the Bolshoi. Lou and Emma sat side by side on the sofa listening to them, while Charlie dozed across both their laps. When he was asleep, Mrs Dillon put him back in his cot and the two girls went out on to the steps to see Jem on his way. It was a cold night, clear and windless, with stars.

Jem wheeled his bike to the foot of the

steps. Looking up at them he said, 'Are you two going to Angela's party then?'

'We haven't decided,' said Lou. 'We might and we might not.'

'Well, let me know,' he said, 'because she's invited me too.' And with that he waved and rode off into the night.

Chapter Eight

All the girls at school were talking about it. Someone knew someone who had seen Jem coming out of Angela's house last Wednesday evening.

'That Angela is his girlfriend,' Melanie told them. 'But she's really snobby and horrible.'

'Well, if you're pretty and you've got lots of money, you don't have to be nice as well,' said Tracey bitterly.

Lou said nothing; she was too angry. The very evening when she had told him how Angela was bullying Emma! He had gone to see her . . . at her house . . . He was even going to her party!

'Lots of money *and* a big, posh house,' said Liza.

They all agreed that boys were the pits.

On the way home, Jem rode ahead with a gang of boys. They looked as though they were teasing him, but he didn't seem to mind. At the corner of her street, Lou found him alone, waiting for her.

'Hi!' he said.

Lou looked at him coldly and walked on without stopping. He rode beside her.

'You're coming to our house tonight,' he said. 'For supper . . . all of you . . .'

Lou had almost forgotten. It was Jem's gran's Caribbean night.

'I may not come,' she said. 'I've got a bad headache,' and she turned away down her basement steps without asking him in.

But she did go. For one thing, she was curious about his home, and for another, she hoped it would annoy Angela to know that she had been there.

Jem's grandad was nice. He had long grey hair tied back in a ponytail, a soft Scottish accent and freckles. He was not at all like Jem except that they were both tall and slim.

The house was full of warmth and colour and music. The food was strange and delicious. Everyone had been invited: the Brownes, the Lamberts and Mrs Dillon. Even Charlie had come along to join the fun. It should have been a wonderful evening, and so it was . . . for everyone except Lou.

Jem asked about her headache. He could

see that she was not in a good mood.

'Headache?' said Jenny, catching the word. 'I didn't know you had a headache, Lou. You should have said.' And then everyone clucked over her. He did that on purpose, she thought furiously, just to show me up. Jem caught her frosty glare, so he went and talked to Emma. And then he went on talking to Emma – all evening. Lou got quite fed up with watching the pair of them jabbering away. Emma was supposed to be her friend. It was true that she did come over and ask if Lou was all right. But Lou couldn't tell her about Jem and Angela, so she just said, 'I'm OK. I don't feel like talking, that's all.'

'I expect you're getting that flu thing,' said Emma kindly. 'I mean, with your headache and everything. You don't look very well.'

Thanks a lot! thought Lou crossly. Not only is everyone ignoring me, but I look awful too! But aloud she just growled, 'Go and talk to Jem . . .' And Emma did.

After supper, they made music. Jem's grandad, whose name was John, played the piano and his gran, Aurelia, known as Orly, was persuaded to sing. Her voice was deep and rich like treacle toffee, but she could also sing high and clear. Then Mrs Dillon announced that she would sing a Russian folk-song. Jem's grandad knew the tune and played for her. The song was slow and tuneful but rather gloomy. Afterwards John played them something a bit livelier on his clarinet.

Then Jem and Emma found that they

both knew the same piano piece and played it as a rather wobbly duet. They were not very good but they got a lot of applause. So Charlie had a go, plonking up and down the keys and being rewarded with lots of kisses. Lou felt really left out. The others smiled at her kindly from time to time. They all thought she was being brave about her headache so as not to spoil the fun. In the end, she really did have a headache. She was glad when it was time to go home.

Emma came to say goodnight.

'What were you and Jem chattering about all evening?' asked Lou.

'He was telling me about his mother,' said Emma.

'So, where is she then?'

'She's in Germany,' said Emma. 'She sings with a group. She travels a lot because of her career. But Jem says he doesn't mind because he's always lived with his gran and grandad.'

Lou really hated it when Emma knew things *she* didn't know.

'Oh, well then,' she said. 'That's all right then, isn't it?'

She sounded irritable and Emma looked at her anxiously. 'I hope you haven't got flu,' she said, 'or we'll miss Angela's party.'

'You could always go with Jem,' said Lou bitterly.

Emma looked shocked. 'Oh, no!' she said. 'I would never go without you!'

Lou felt a bit better.

Chapter Nine

'Does Angela live with her grandfather?' asked Mrs Browne. She was driving Lou and Emma to the party.

'Yes,' said Emma. 'Her grandmother died a few years ago, so Angela's mother runs the house.'

'What about her father?'

'He left home when Angela was quite small,' said Emma.

'Oh, how sad!' said Mrs Browne.

Now Emma even knew things about *Angela* that Lou didn't know. It was very annoying . . .

'This must be it,' said Mrs Browne. 'What a lovely house!' She parked at the foot of the elegant steps and the girls jumped out. 'Have a good time,' she called as she drove off.

'Fat chance!' said Lou, who wasn't looking forward to watching Angela swanning about and showing off.

But Emma was starry-eyed. 'Oh, Lou!' she said. 'I'm sure it's going to be fun!'

The front door stood open and they could hear shrieks of laughter. A young woman greeted them and took their coats.

The noise was coming from the back of the house, where a bouncy castle had

been set up. It wasn't big enough for
everyone, so her friends were watching
while Angela jumped up and down. With
her was Jem and *three other boys from Lou's
school*! Lou was outraged; this was

poaching of the worst kind!

Angela looked as though she was having a great time. Her face was flushed and her blonde hair was flying. She seemed to go out of her way to bump into Jem and he didn't seem to mind. Angela's friends greeted Emma with sugary sweetness; they ignored Lou.

This is going to be too awful, she thought. Maybe I could sneak off home when no one is looking.

She felt a hand on her shoulder and, turning, saw Angela's grandfather. He beckoned her into a book-lined room.

'I need some help from my favourite Rat,' he said. 'I'm doing some magic tricks after tea and Angela was going to help me. Now she says she won't do it. She wants to stay with her new friend –

some boy, I think – so I need a new assistant.'

'Oh, great!' said Lou. Now it wouldn't be boring. 'What will I have to do?' she asked eagerly.

'Just hand me some props,' said the Wind-up Merchant, 'look after the rabbits I pull out of hats . . . oh, and at the end I make you disappear.'

'Disappear!' said Lou. 'Is this a wind-up?'

Angela's grandfather laughed. 'Cross my heart,' he said. 'I've hired a real vanishing cabinet.'

'Brilliant!' said Lou. 'I don't suppose there's a costume too?'

'Chosen for Angela, so it should fit you. I've got robes and a turban and you've got . . .'

'Veils and things?' said Lou eagerly.

'Got it in one!' said the Wind-up Merchant.

A tall, very thin woman came in. Lou could see at once that she was Angela's mother. 'Will she do it?' the woman asked.

'Oh, yes!' said Lou. 'I mean . . . I really love magic.'

'How kind,' said the woman without enthusiasm. 'Maria will bring you to my room after tea and I will help you dress.' She smiled politely and went out again.

'We'll need a rehearsal,' said the Wind-up Merchant. 'Do you mind missing the bouncy castle?'

'Oh, no!' said Lou. 'I think they're a bit childish.'

They practised all the tricks, including

the marvellous vanishing cabinet. The rabbit wasn't real but you could make its ears wiggle. Lou decided to be the best magic assistant ever.

There was a splendid tea and Emma came to sit next to her. 'Where have you been?' she asked. 'I couldn't find you anywhere.'

'It's a secret,' said Lou. 'You'll find out later.'

She felt a bit mean, but Emma *had* left her for her new schoolfriends. After tea the others went to watch cartoons on a huge video screen.

Maria, the young woman who had taken their coats, appeared from nowhere and led Lou up to a luxurious bedroom where Angela's mother was waiting. The costume was fabulous: harem pants, embroidered slippers with turned-up toes and a top decorated with shining beads. There was even a jewelled headdress and a veil which showed only her eyes. Angela's mother added some eye make-up.

There were pictures in Lou's ballet book of a dancer in a costume just like it. Lou longed to dance in it.

'Perfect,' said the Wind-up Merchant when he saw her.

'You look pretty good too,' said Lou, admiring his magician's robes and the turban with a huge jewel in it.

The magic had been set up in another room with special coloured lighting. The audience sat on the thick carpet. There

268

was Eastern music and Lou appeared in a puff of smoke when the Magician waved his hand. Everyone gasped and Lou got carried away. She improvised a swaying dance and the audience clapped and cheered.

'You're upstaging me again,' hissed the Magician, but Lou could see that he was laughing. She went a bit over the top, dancing on and off with the props and making the rabbit's ears wiggle like mad. The vanishing cabinet was a great success, with Lou disappearing and reappearing in puffs of coloured smoke.

The applause at the end was deafening. The Magician waved his hand in front of Lou's face and removed her veil so that they could see who it was. Jem was clapping as hard as he could, while Angela sat stony-faced beside him, her hands hardly moving at all. Serve her right, thought Lou, for letting her grandfather down.

There was a disco after the magic. Lou wished she could keep the costume on, but it was only hired and a bit fragile for disco-dancing. But even in her own clothes she found herself the centre of attention. Jem danced with Angela but the others clustered around Lou. They wanted to know how the tricks were done, but Lou had promised not to tell.

The party ended with fireworks in the garden. They watched from the terrace but it was spoilt for Lou when every burst of light and colour showed Jem still right by Angela's side. I don't care. I don't *care*! Lou told herself. If he is stupid enough to want to be Angela's friend, she can jolly well have him!

Chapter Ten

The next day seemed very dull. It was Sunday and Emma had gone with her parents to visit her granny in Worthing. Jenny was busy with her evening-class homework, Charlie was having his afternoon nap and Lou was really bored. There was a knock at the door.

'Get that, will you, Lou?' called Jenny.

It was Jem.

Lou glared at him. 'Angela let you off

your lead, has she?' she said frostily.

'Don't be like that, Lou,' said Jem. 'Do you want to come down to the park?'

Lou did, but she was also pretty angry with him. She wavered for a minute, then called, 'I'm going to the park with Jem, Mum.'

'Be back by four,' called her mother.

As they went Jem said, 'The magic was great. I really like Angela's grandad.'

'So do I,' said Lou.

'You looked great,' said Jem.

'With a veil over my face, you mean?'

Jem laughed. 'With or without,' he said.

The park was cold and deserted. Lou sat on the damp roundabout while Jem pushed it round.

'I did a deal with Angela', he said, 'after you told me about Emma.'

Lou said nothing.

'I told her I would only go to her party if you and Emma were there . . .'

Still Lou said nothing.

'And that if they were nice to Em at school, I would bring three other boys to the party with me.'

'You sold out,' said Lou coldly.

'Well . . . sort of,' said Jem cheerfully, 'and she drove a hard bargain! She made me promise to stay next to her all through the party.'

'You're pathetic,' said Lou.

'But it worked,' said Jem. 'It worked better than you yelling at her. Em had a great time and the others are getting to know her.'

'It won't last,' said Lou.

'Maybe . . . Maybe not.'

As they walked back, Jem said, 'There's worse that I haven't told you.'

Lou wasn't sure that she wanted to hear.

'I didn't just do it for Emma,' he said. 'It was for me too. Everyone knows that

Angela has amazing parties and the other boys all wanted to go. They think she's great. I was the one who could get them invited. I was the one she talked to all evening. It made me look good.'

'You slimeball!' said Lou, grinning.

'Aren't I just!' He grinned back. 'A boy who does ballet', he explained, 'has to work hard at his image!'

'You mean he needs to be friends with the most popular girl?'

'It helps.'

There was a long silence.

'So why are you here?' asked Lou. 'Why aren't you round at Angela's?'

'Ah, well,' said Jem. 'It was your magic dancing. The others think you're the flavour of the month now . . .'

He ducked as she went to hit him and

she had to chase him the rest of the way
home.

But she hadn't quite forgiven him. He
shouldn't have done it without her
knowing. She needed to talk about it and
she couldn't tell Emma. So that night

when she went to bed, she told her
mother.

'It was kind of him to want to help
Emma,' said Jenny.

'He did it for himself too!'

'We all do things for ourselves.'

'But he should have told *me* what he
was doing! I mean, Emma is *my* friend.'

'She is his friend too.'

There was a long silence. Then her
mother said, 'Friendship is a sort of
network, Lou. It links us all to one
another. But a net is not a web with one
person in the centre, knowing what all
the others do, pulling all the strings.'

'But, Mum, the others . . . they're not
really Emma's friends,' protested Lou.
'Not like I am. They just pretend to be
nice to her when Angela tells them to.'

'Do you think Emma doesn't know that? Do you think she can't tell real friends from fake ones?'

Lou thought about it. She knew how badly Emma wanted to fit in at school. She might want it enough to fool herself. Suppose she settled for being one of Angela's cronies? Lou sighed. But her mother was right about the web. That was just the sort of friendship Angela offered. She sat in the centre of her web like a rich, fat spider. When she moved, the whole web shook and all her friends jumped about. And now she had fixed her sticky little threads on to Emma and Jem and she was starting to reel them in . . .

Lou really liked this image. She pictured Angela's face on a little fat body with lots of legs sticking out . . .

Well, she won't get me, she thought. And she won't get Jem and Emma, not if I can help it . . . But she didn't know what she was going to do about it.

'Maybe you just have to trust Emma,' said Jenny, as if she read Lou's thoughts. 'I think you will always be her best friend.'

She hugged Lou and kissed her goodnight. Lou hugged her back. As she snuggled down under her quilt, her mother paused in the doorway. 'And that boy isn't stupid,' she said. 'I think he can tell who his real friends are.' Then she switched out the light.

Lou dozed in the dark and thought about it. She wasn't so sure . . . about Jem not being stupid . . . After all, he did say he might decide to become a footballer . . . She would have to stay friends with him, just to make sure he didn't . . . He was such a good dancer . . . and ballet needed all the boys it could get.